"Attention, motorist!" Blondel's dash radio said. *"Please pull to the right shoulder and stop your machine."*

Blondel hunched down over the wheel and floorboarded the Mustang. It jumped ahead, snarled under the helicopter close enough to buck in the backwash from the rotors, roared ahead.

"Sir," the radio chided him gently, *"it will be to your advantage to comply voluntarily with all instructions."*

Blondel ignored the order, swung a wide curve in a squeal of tortured rubber—and abruptly the engine died.

THE MONITORS

THE MONITORS

KEITH LAUMER

A TOM DOHERTY ASSOCIATES BOOK

THE MONITORS

This is a work of fiction. All the characters and events portrayed in this book are fictional, and any resemblance to real people or incidents is purely coincidental.

Copyright © 1966 by Keith Laumer

A TOR Book

Published by:

Tom Doherty Associates, Inc.
8-10 West 36th Street
New York, New York 10018

First TOR printing: May 1984

ISBN: 812-54-369-6
Can. Ed.: 812-54-370-X

Cover art by: Hannah M.G. Shapero

Printed in the United States of America

To Harlan Ellison
in spite of his many virtues

CHAPTER ONE

It was a warm afternoon in the city. A fitful wind whirled its burden of gaily-colored aspirin and tranquilizer cartons and gum and cigarette wrappers into the faces of the well-fed burghers and their mates who puffed along on bunioned feet, their life-blunted features set in expressions of opaque anonymity, oblivious of the mixed chorus of auto horns, the spirited cries of impatient taxi drivers, and the merry voices of news vendors hawking details of the latest disaster.

Ace Blondel stood before a shop window, idly noting the temperature of the pavement through his thinning shoesoles and admiring a display of hand-painted neckties, glossy cardboard shoes and sports coats nattily fashioned of lightweight burlap stiffened with glucose, all marked down—according to attached placards—from formerly incredible sums in honor of National Easy Payment Week. In the dusty glass he saw the reflection of the busy street, the mismatched building fronts across the way with their clustered signboards thrusting for favored placement like jungle foliage fighting for survival, and, above, a narrow strip of smoke-dimmed blue sky.

He turned in time to confront a nubile wench with lust-red lips, bosoms thrust up and forward like fruits offered on a tray, her one-piece pelvis clamped in a corset as rigid as armor plate. His tentative smile died at birth, impaled by the kind of look reserved in other cultures for convicted rapists. He sighed philosophically, glanced at his seven-jewel wrist watch, and headed for the painted-over glass door of Harry's Marine Bar and Grill.

Inside, a television set above the long bar made sounds like a lovelorn elk, shedding its flickering glow on extinct fishermen's nets, crumbling cork floats, a mummified tuna with a brass plate celebrating its capture, and a hand-painted mural representing extravagantly mammalian mermaids, their charms ignored by a pair of regulars perched on stools like jockeys waiting for the bell that never comes.

A large man with a white apron tied high over a massive paunch paused in his glass polishing, shifted his toothpick, and called: "Ace! Welcome home, pal! What'll it be?"

"Just squeeze me one out of the bar rag, Harry." Blondel slid onto a stool as far as possible from the sound of the telly. "That's all the budget allows for the present."

"Broke again, pal?" The bartender shifted the toothpick again, leaned on the bar with an elbow the size of a ham hock. "I thought you had a swell job with the Health and Welfare Department airlifting encyclopedias to them underprivileged Bulgarians."

"It was the Cambodians; and it wasn't encyclopedias—it was movie magazines. And it was the US Information Service, not HEW. And as of last week I don't have the job."

"What happened?"

"Somebody discovered the funny books were Red Chinese propaganda. A fink in the translating department, they figure. They washed out the program, and me with it."

"Tough," Harry commiserated. "Why don't you sign on regular with one of the airlines, Ace? With your experience you'd be a cinch."

"Not for me, Harry. The hours wouldn't suit me."

"What hours? I got a brother-in-law flies one day, off three—"

"Regular hours. Also regular schedules and regular forms to fill out—"

"And regular pay checks." Harry did things with bottles and glasses, put a drink in front of Blondel.

"What I'd do if I was your age, Ace, I'd

head for Ecuador. I heard a guy can make a fortune down there now, with this revolution they got coming up."

"A misnomer," one of the drinkers called from his end of the bar. "What we call revolutions are merely the normal Latin method of holding elections. That is to say, bullets are as good as ballots and much more easily counted. Now—"

"Nix, Prof. Ya wanna get us all picked up for some kind of Reds?" his drinking partner protested. They went on with the discussion. Blondel used the first half of the drink.

"Hey, Harry. I said the pink label stuff . . ."

"Too hot for rot-gut." Harry leaned confidentially close. "You know what I think? I think the whole world situation's a deal Washington cooked up with the Rooshians to like simulate the economy—" He stopped talking and cocked his head at the TV set. The musical adenoids had stopped and an eerie whistling of the sort usually associated with mad scientists was modulating up and down the scale. The screen flashed solid white, then zigzags began running across it from right to left. The zigzags blinked out and circles started whirling up out of the center of the screen.

"What's this, some new kind of commercial?" The Prof's buddy sounded grieved.

"That set ain't given me any trouble before." Harry went to stand in front of it.

"It's these noocular bombs they're testing," he stated positively. "The weather—"

"*Attention,*" a strong, he-man voice said from the TV. "*Your attention please! An announcement of vital importance will be made in five minutes. All persons are requested to go at once to a radio or television set and stand by. Attention! An announcement of vital importance . . .*"

There were echoes from outside; the voice was coming in strongly on a distant PA system. Harry reached for the volume, turned it down—but the voice continued loud and clear. Harry flipped the set off; there was a click. But the voice kept on: "*. . . stand by! An announcement of vital importance . . .*"

"I knew they'd pull one like this some day." Harry was snapping the switch on and off with a sound like a ping-pong match. "Commercials you can't turn off, yet! I got a good mind—"

"Now, Harry," the Prof said. "Don't do anything hasty." He was frowning fixedly at the set. "Try pulling the plug."

"Yeah." Harry yanked the cord from the wall. The voice went on; the blooping circles threw spooky light on the Prof's face.

"*. . . importance will be made in four minutes! Your attention please! All persons are requested . . .*"

Muttering, Harry reached up, seized the set in a bearhug and hauled it down from its shelf, deposited it heavily on the bar. He slapped the top and sides. The voice bobbled and went on: "*. . . to the nearest radio or television set and stand by. Your attention, please. . . .*"

"Enough's enough already!" Harry swept the set off behind the bar with a crash like an airliner hitting a mountainside. Light flashed once, brightly, and went out. The voice cut off in mid-word.

"*. . . vital importance.*" the PA system outside boomed, "*. . . three minutes . . .*"

"Harry, you shouldn't have done that," Prof said unhappily. "The phenomenon—"

"You can still hear it." Harry waved an arm. "I give up!" He stepped over the wreckage, grabbed a glass and began polishing furiously.

"What was the guy selling?" Prof's buddy asked.

"Who cares?" Harry barked. "Laxatives? Deodorant? Hell, what's wrong with smelling natural? A new kind of toilet paper that'll revolutionize the art? Some kind of reducing pills that'll take it off faster than you can pack it on eating the stuff the other commercials are selling? The latest ten-porthole gas-eater with built-in metal-fatigue—?"

"Maybe we ought to listen," Blondel said. "It might be important."

"Hah!" Harry snorted, but he was listening now. Outside, the PA sounded louder than ever. A siren was howling somewhere, getting closer.

"*. . . one minute,*" the big voice was saying, "*Attention . . .*" Blondel slid off the stool and went to the door, pushed out onto the sidewalk. Pedestrians had halted, stood with their mouths hanging open, craning to see where the voice was coming from. A small bald-headed man ran from a TV repair shop across the street, holding his hands over his ears.

"You don't suppose," the Prof said thoughtfully from behind Blondel, "that every set in his shop . . . ?"

A police car swung around the corner, the siren moaning down the scale as it pulled to the curb in front of the bar. Two cops hopped out and heavyfooted it across to the TV store.

"Stand by for the announcement—NOW!" The combined volume of every set in the neighborhood blasted out loud enough to rattle windows. It was quiet then for a few seconds except for the sounds of police voices raised in inquiry.

"Somehow, Mr. Blondel," Prof said, "I have a feeling that this is more than a mere advertising stunt. . . ."

"Citizens of Earth," a new voice racketed across the street. *"I am the Tersh Jetterax. It is my pleasure to announce to you that a new government has now taken over the conduct of all public affairs. Effective at once, all former police, military, judiciary, and legislative functions are suspended. Any individual previously serving in any official capacity whatever may consider himself at liberty. Monitors who will assume the administration of the*

new system will arrive among you momentarily. They will be distinguished by uniforms of a distinctive yellow color, and will take full responsibility for the maintenance of law and order. Essential personnel such as medical doctors, bus drivers, maintenance specialists, et cetera, are requested to carry on temporarily, until relieved. All other citizens are to go at once to their places of residence and await further instructions."

As the speech ended, there was a blood-curdling yell. The Prof grabbed Blondel's arm and pointed. Something huge was settling down over the building tops: a gold-painted blimp, half the size of the Hindenburg, unadorned except for a curlicue of black lines near one end. It dropped in fast, maneuvered past the jungle of antennae on top of Levi's, lowered itself down between the buildings until it was hovering ten feet above the street, as big as a beached ocean liner. People were scattering, running away from it; a high, wailing sound was coming up from the crowd. Heads were popping from windows all up and down the street.

"My God, they're everywhere!" Prof pointed. There were other blimps in the distance drifting down as light as dandelion feathers. One sailed in from a side street, came to rest half a dozen blocks above where Blondel watched.

"What ... what's it all about?" Harry's bull-tones had lost their assurance.

"There is no cause for alarm," the original

voice racketed over the confusion. *"Please follow all instructions quickly and without disorder. . . ."*

The blimp, filling the street before the bar, hung just above the tops of a pack of stalled automobiles whose drivers had abandoned them and run when the shadow settled over them. Now panels flopped open near the bottom of the immense airship. Men in gleaming gold uniforms emerged at a jog trot. They were tall fellows with physiques like lifeguards. They spread out, started directing traffic, shooing pedestrians along the sidewalk, helping old ladies cross the street.

The four policemen emerged from the TV repair shop, gaped at the scene, then whipped out whistles and blew piercing blasts. One clamped a large hand on a passing yellow-clad shoulder. The Monitor waved a hand. The cop stiffened; then he took off his cap, tossed it in the gutter, dropped his badge beside it, then wandered away into the crowd. The other three cops fared no better.

"It's the Rooshians," Harry groaned. "The bums got the jump on us!"

"A power seizure—an invasion—carried out in broad daylight!" the Prof gasped.

One of the Monitors was standing ten feet from them, a Captain Video in gilt long-johns, making a nice little bow to a well-shaped redhead.

"No cause for alarm, ma'am," he was

saying. His voice sounded like the announcer's. "Go to your home, please, and—"

"Whatta ya yakking, go home?" She had a voice like a dry bearing. "I'm onna way to the byooty shop! I got a appointment, for a week, already. Outa my way, ya bum!" She swung a pocketbook the size of first base at the invader's head.

The blow failed to connect. The swing skidded off into a vague kind of wave. The redhead's mouth opened, but no sound came out. Then she turned and trotted back the way she had come. The Monitor turned toward Blondel.

"Gentlemen, please move along now to your respective domiciles." He showed a nice smile, all square chin and curly blond hair and shiny white teeth.

"The hell you say." Harry pushed past Blondel, paunchy but with adequate muscle under the fat. "Who do you Reds think you're pushing around—" He reached for the man in yellow, who leaned aside just far enough and did something quick with his hands. Harry hadn't been touched, but he came to a stop, swung around with a bewildered look on his face, then started off docilely up the street.

"Hey, where's he going?" the Prof's pal asked.

"Home," Blondel guessed. "Just like the man said." He took the Prof's arm, eased him back toward the door.

"Please go along to your homes now,

gentlemen." The Monitor was still using the toothpaste smile.

"Sure," Blondel said. "We live here. Rooms in back, you know." He backed through the door into the bar, eased the door shut.

"Hey, what's—?" the Prof's friend started.

"Quiet, Freddy." The Prof gave Blondel a sharp look. "What now, Mr. Blondel?"

He went to the window and looked out past the cardboard cutout of a blonde model holding a beer stein. A squad of ten or twelve of the men in yellow had formed a column of twos and were heading off down the block. More of them were filing out of the blimp, lining up, moving out. Most of the local citizens were on the move now, looking back over their shoulders as they went.

"Ah-hah!" The Prof's friend pointed across the street. A squad of invaders were moving in through the wide-open doors of the First National. "Now I get it!"

"This is more than a bank job," Blondel said, watching another crew marching up the post office steps. "These boys mean business. Did you see the way they handled Harry?"

"How did these bums catch SAC with its pants down, after all the dough—"

"Calmly, Freddy, calmly," the Prof soothed. "Do you suppose they're Russians?" he asked Blondel.

"Try the phone; call the *Times*. Maybe they know what's going on."

"It took some brains to plan this caper,"

Freddy opined, "I didn't think them Ruskies had it in 'em."

The Prof returned from his errand. "A recorded message," he said. " 'Stand by your radio or TV for the next announcement.' Same thing when I tried the television station."

"Did you see them cops?" Freddy inquired. "They acted like they was getting their twenty-year gold watches from the mayor."

"Look, fellows." Blondel chewed his lip, watching the last of the golden-hued troops disembarking from the blimp, still hanging lightly above the stalled cars, its belly sweeping down like a circus big top, closing off the sky. "They've stopped coming. It looks like there are only a couple hundred of them."

"Per blimp," Prof amended. "And we don't know how many blimps."

"That ain't many—not for a town this size," Freddy stated belligerently. "Let's rush 'em!"

"Wait a minute," Blondel demurred. "Let's not do anything hasty."

"He's right, Freddy," Prof agreed. "That airship—it doesn't quite fit in with what I've understood of the scope and sophistication of Soviet technology. . . ."

"So they was holding out on us." Freddy dismissed the objection. "I say let's jump 'em fast and show the bums they can't just walk in and take over, even if SAC is asleep at the switch!"

"This is no time for dramatics." Blondel turned to face the others. "Men, we've got to evade their dragnet and join up with an organized Underground!"

"Nuts! I got a good mind to—"

"Freddy," Prof silenced him.

"We'll have to sneak out the back way," Blondel planned aloud. "Once clear of the city, we can make contact—"

"How?" Prof interrupted.

"Hey!" Freddy said brightly. "Keen! We'll go into some little like tavern in some hick town, and there'll be some beautiful dames and some old peasant types sitting around, and we'll give the password or something. . . ."

"Ummm. Too risky," Prof demurred. "They might turn out to be counterintelligence agents. I'm too old to perform well under torture."

"Gee, yeah, you're right," Freddy conceded. "We might break and spill the whereabouts of the secret headquarters, or something."

"What secret headquarters?" Blondel demanded.

"I said, or something!" Freddy returned.

"Look, we can worry about contacting the Resistance later." Blondel cut the discussion short. "Right now, we have to get clear of the city."

"Don't you imagine the *coup* embraces a wider area than the metropolitan district?" Prof sounded doubtful.

"Maybe—but let's not think negatively.

We'll have to pack a few iron rations and possibly some brandy, as a stimulant. . . ."

"Why not just, er, depart openly?"

"Are you kidding? What kind of Underground activity would that be?"

"Sorry," Prof murmured.

"I don't guess we need to blacken our faces," Blondel mused. "I guess we could snitch a couple of ice picks from back of the bar for weapons."

"I got this bad wrist," Freddy said.

"Perhaps we'd better stand by and see what develops," the Prof offered. "Probably our forces are on the way even now; any abrupt moves on our part might merely complicate matters."

"And be trapped here?"

". . . *remain in your homes,*" the voice of the Monitor boomed from the street. *"Further instructions will be issued shortly. . . ."*

"Ah . . ." The Prof tugged at his stiff collar. "I think perhaps, on the whole, it might be better to do as they say—"

"What? Take orders from some interloper you didn't even get a chance to vote for?" Blondel expostulated.

"I've been voting losing tickets for some decades," Prof said mildly.

"Well, suit yourself," Blondel said. "Freddy and I will just have to try it alone."

"I got this back, too," Freddy said. "Ask Prof, he'll tell you." Freddy put a hand on his hip and arched his back, registering pain stoically endured.

"You mean both of you are going to just sit here and let this ... this *invasion* happen without lifting a finger?"

"No!" Freddy declared. He went to the bar, poured out drinks all around, tossed his back. "Ahhh ..." he said, and patted his stomach.

"Well, it looks like I'll have to contact the loyalists on my own," Blondel said. He looked expectantly at the others. They looked back.

"Well," Blondel added. "I guess I'd better get moving. It'll be dark in seven or eight hours."

"Yeah," Freddy nodded. "Maybe six and a half."

"If they should, ah, apprehend you," Prof cautioned, "tell them whatever they want to know. Don't worry about us."

"Yeah, we'll hold the fort back here." Freddy squared his shoulders.

"I mean, if you *want* me to wait a while ..." Blondel said.

"The sooner you make your try the better chance you got," Freddy said. "When you get through, tell 'em me and Prof is standing by our posts, come what may."

"I mean, if you really think I'd be jeopardizing the defense effort—" Blondel paused expectantly.

"Go get 'em, Tiger," Freddy said, and hiccupped.

"Each man to his own chosen duty." Prof

clapped Blondel on the shoulder. "We'll think none the less of you for it."

"Hey, *I'm* the one that's going on the dangerous mission," Blondel objected.

"As to that, who's to say?" Prof said wisely, and handed his glass to Freddy for a refill.

"A guy could take offense at a crack like that," Freddy said darkly.

"If he didn't have a bad wrist!" Blondel snapped. "Well, so long, fellows. See you in a concentration camp." He went to the bar, slipped a fifth of green-label into his side pocket, and soft-footed it to the door at the back.

At the end of the alley Blondel peered out at a milling throng of citizens among whom the tall, smiling figures of the Monitors moved confidently, giving instructions, shaping up the crowd, visibly bringing order out of chaos.

"Are *you* saved, son?" a loud voice boomed at Blondel's elbow. He started violently, turned to face a chubby-jowled, florid-faced man in soiled cuffs and a drab suit of unfashionable cut.

"Well, I'm working on it," Blondel countered. "But keep your voice down—"

"Have you taken thought for your soul this morning?" the stranger pressed on. "How do you stand up in Heaven?"

"Right now I'm more concerned about my neck," Blondel said impatiently. A finger like a Polish sausage shot out to point at Blondel's chin. "Son, I'm going to pretend you never said that! Now let's pray a few words—"

"Pardon me." Blondel side-stepped him. "I'm in a hurry—"

The finger hooked his lapel. "In too big a hurry to hear the word of God?"

"Sorry; I didn't recognize you. Look—"

"*You* look, son! Ah, they are arriven among us! Down on your knees, boy!—"

Blondel fended off the heavy hands that had landed on his shoulders.

"Look, I have things to do—"

"Behold the angels of the Lord!" The hands gripped him, aimed him toward the street. "There they are, wearing their golden raiment! Ah, rejoice, son, for they have come to bring the heavenly light to us sinners!"

"Speak for yourself, pops," Blondel retorted. "Personally, I take a different view of matters—"

"How's that! You utter defiance of the Lord?" The hands jumped to Blondel's throat; they were large, horny hands, and they closed with the force of grappling hooks. Blondel brought his clasped fists up in a swing that broke the hold, simultaneously ramming a knee into the evangelist's midriff. The latter doubled over, clutching himself.

"Praise God!" he shouted. "Just wait till I get unfolded here, you shifty son of a spotted pup," he added in a lower tone, "and I'll bend you into a pretzel."

Blondel sidled past him, stepped out, and

mingled with the crowd. Some of the herded citizens, he noted, seemed bewildered, moving along in a state of shock. Others, wearing expressions of mild interest, craned for a better view of the yellow-clad VIP's. At a street corner, Blondel paused while a minor traffic jam was sorted out by efficient Monitors.

". . . told the old lady they was soft on Communism . . ." a fat man was saying.

". . . been expecting it for weeks," a wizened old fellow stated. "My wife's cousin is a big shot in the Job Corps . . ."

". . . cute bunch of guys, but they're all so *butch* . . ."

". . . college-educated radicals sold us out . . ."

A trim, yellow-clad young fellow appeared, urging the bystanders along. Blondel attempted to fade back, found himself facing the Monitor, who nodded pleasantly and said, "If you'll just stand by, sir, special transportation facilities will be in operation in a few minutes."

"Yeah, uh, I was just ducking over to Aunt Gertie's for some plum preserves," Blondel improvised. "But it can wait. . . ."

"Your address, sir?"

"Ah, I don't actually have one—that is, I'm just visiting—I mean, I live right down the street."

"Please go to your home on foot, in that case, sir." The Monitor smiled disarmingly.

"The confusion will be cleared up shortly, and normal movement can be resumed."

"Sure. . . ." Blondel backed into the throng, feeling eyes boring into his back. He cut down a side street, emerged on a less densely packed thoroughfare. Monitors were on duty here too, directing traffic, herding the pedestrians. The big voice was still blaring out instructions, almost unnoticed over the crowd babble.

There was a gray Mustang parked at the curb; there was no one near it at the moment. The keys were in the ignition, Blondel noted. He rounded the front bumper, tried the door. It opened. He slid in behind the wheel, tried the starter. The engine kicked off with an unselfconscious roar. Blondel wheeled the small car away from the curb. None of the Monitors seemed to notice.

Blondel drove carefully, passed block after block of Monitor-occupied territory. As he neared the city's edge, traffic slowed to a crawl. Ahead he saw a barricade across the street, manned by two Monitors. Blondel noted that they were waving most of the cars back. His turn came. A face as bland as an insurance salesman's at renewal time bent over and looked in the window.

"Where are you bound, sir?"

"Home," Blondel said cheerfully. "Just like you boys said."

"Where do you reside, sir?"

"Hah?"

"Where is your home, please?"

"That way." Blondel pointed ahead.

"Very well, sir. Kindly go directly there and remain by your radio or—"

"Yeah, television." Blondel favored the invader with a grin, wink, and chuckle. "I've been listening to you boys. I got the message, yes siree!"

"Thank you, sir. Please remain on the main route."

"Ah . . . suppose I, ah, sort of wandered off it?"

There was no visible change in the Monitor's expression, but suddenly it seemed to penetrate like a laser beam.

"Like, if I got lost," Blondel amplified, feeling the grin going sick on his face.

"Take care not to get lost, sir. It would create unnecessary confusion."

"Yeah, sure thing, chief."

The Monitor waved him on. His grin dropped as soon as he was past the barrier. It was nothing specific that the Monitor had said or done, but Blondel was aware of a feeling under his ribs as though he had been playing Russian roulette with all nine chambers loaded.

Twenty minutes later, with the city lights aglow far behind the racing Mustang, a noise like a giant eggbeater penetrated over the hum of the car engine. Blondel ducked down and squinted up through the windshield. A small helicopter was swinging across the road ahead, dropping in quickly to intercept him. It was bright gold in color.

"Attention, motorist!" Blondel's dash radio said in a kindly tenor. *"Please pull to the right shoulder and stop your machine."*

Blondel hunched down over the wheel and floorboarded the Mustang. It jumped ahead, snarled under the helicopter close enough to buck in the backwash from the rotors, roared ahead, wide open. A moment later the copter reappeared off to the side at about fifty feet altitude.

"Please stop your machine," the radio said calmly, *"Don't be alarmed. This is not an arrest, merely a routine counselling action."*

Blondel's weight was on the gas pedal. The needle wavered up past a hundred, to a hundred and ten Detroit, which he estimated should mean a good eighty-five actual. The heli was still loafing along beside him.

"Sir," the radio chided him gently, *"please bring your auto to a halt at once. It will be to your advantage to comply voluntarily with all instructions."*

Blondel ignored the order, swung a wide curve in a squeal of tortured rubber—and abruptly the engine died. Blondel wrestled the suddenly stiff wheel, saw the copter swinging across directly in front of him. A small puff of smoke jetted from an orifice on its underside, expanded quickly to a pinkish cloud that enveloped the car. He sniffed once, caught the first hint of a crushed cherry flavor, and slammed the air intakes shut.

Then he aimed the slowing car straight down the center of the road and flopped over on the wheel as realistically as comfort allowed. The car rolled on; there were a number of preliminary thumps, then a hard dip and lurch, and the car slowed to a stop. Blondel lay limp across the wheel, hearing the *whap-whap* of the copter growing louder, feeling the car rock as the copter settled in beside it. The noise of the rotors braked down and ceased. There were faint sounds of opening hatches, then the crunch of feet on hard ground.

Blondel opened one eye. The copter was parked twenty feet away, dead ahead. Two Monitors were walking back toward him, tall and trim in yellow. He waited until they were opposite the front bumper, then reached for the switch. The engine caught; he threw the transmission into low, gunned straight ahead. The two men in yellow jumped aside. The wheels screamed on turf. Blondel cut the wheel hard, felt the car skid sideways; it struck the stern of the heli a solid clip, kept going in a hail of gold plastic chips. The Mustang banged down through the ditch, smashed through rusted barbed wire, clipped off a 666 sign and was back on the pavement, laying rubber all the way up to ninety-five. In the rear-view mirror Blondel saw the two Monitors standing in the middle of the road, looking after him.

CHAPTER TWO

Twenty minutes later, Blondel swung a curve that afforded him a view of gas stations and motels and a clock tower in the distance—and the big gold bulge of a blimp swelling up above a row of red-and-green-shingled housetops. He took the first right, went four blocks to a wire fence lining a field of dry cornstalks, turned left again—and saw the police car blocking the road ahead. Blondel swore silently and pulled off on the right shoulder. The patrol car was a regulation State Patrol Chevrolet, but with a gold skunk-stripe painted down the back. Two yellow uniforms emerged from it, came up, one on either side of the Mustang, looking like fraternity brothers of the last pair he had seen at close range, complete with confident smiles. He cranked the window down.

"Say, those are right pretty new uniforms you fellows are wearing." He took the offensive. "How much did they cost the taxpayers?"

"Thank you for stopping, sir." The Monitor gave Blondel a two-fingered salute and a neat little smile. Cool blue eyes flicked over the inside of the car, "The uniforms are provided by the Authority. All taxes have been voided, retroactive to last midnight, as you perhaps—"

"Yeah, that's a cute one." Blondel nodded as if in agreement with a jest. "That'll be the day. Ah . . . was I doing something wrong, officer?"

"This is merely a routine counselling check, sir. May I have your ignition key?"

"My keys? Maybe I'd better see a badge first. I mean, what are you boys, some kind of special deputies or something?"

"We're your Monitors, sir. You've heard the announcements during the last eighty minutes." It was not a question.

"Ah . . . my radio's on the blink—"

"Testing—one, two, three, four," the radio said clearly,

"Well, can you beat that . . . ?"

"Will you step out of the car, please, sir?" The Monitor opened the door.

"What for?" Blondel demanded. "What did I do . . . ?"

A tingly feeling went over Blondel; his

muscles twitched; his left leg slid out and felt for the ground. He was leaning, sliding across the seat, grabbing the door for support, standing up—with no more volition on his part than it took to fall off a cliff.

"Heyyy . . ." The quaver in his voice was real.

"Don't be alarmed, sir. But all instructions of Monitors must be compiled with promptly, you know."

"What is this? I'm an American citizen! What's this all about?"

"American and other national citizenships have been voided," the Monitor said as casually as if he were giving directions to the men's room. "All citizens of the planet now enjoy equal status before the Authority."

The other Monitor had walked to the back of the car. He stood there, looking at the license plate in an offhand way. Blondel felt his stomach tightening.

"Sir," the Monitor said reproachfully, "thirty-seven minutes ago you were requested to stop for Monitors' counselling, but instead you damaged their vehicle and fled. Please tell me why you did this."

"Well, it was like this," Blondel said hastily. "I thought they were stick-up men."

"The vehicle you are driving is registered in the name of Mr. Chico Y. Lipschultz," the Monitor stated. "Have you his permission to make use of the vehicle?"

"Sure, good old Chick lets me take it any time I like."

"I'll have to ask you to accompany us into the village," the Monitor said. "I'll arrange for the return of the auto to Mr. Lipschultz."

"What about my date? She'll be expecting me, and has she got a temper!"

The Monitor gave Blondel a sad look, as though he were mildly disappointed. He stepped back, and Blondel went along to the patrol car without any heelkicking.

They rode in silence for five minutes, past the assortment of Flats Fixed, Clean Rooms, and Good Eats signs that adorned the approaches to the town. Ahead, a heavy-duty traffic light dangled over an intersection; it changed just as the car reached it. The Monitor at the wheel worked the stick shift awkwardly, braked. The car bucked, and for an instant his eyes flicked down toward the dash. Blondel reached, grabbed the man's yellow pillbox cap and yanked it down hard over his face, then whirled for the door just in time to meet the other Monitor diving forward. The latter bounced backward into his seat. Blondel shook his head, then slammed the door open and was out and running.

A pair of whiskery citizens in soiled undershirts and lived-in overalls gave Blondel the full benefit of four bloodshot eyeballs as he raced past them, but the shock was insufficient to unhook their thumbs from their shoulder-straps. There was an alley ahead; Blondel cut into it, picked out a gray board fence fronting it thirty feet along, made a running jump and got a grip on the top board just before it gave way. He struck on his back with the approximate impact of Steve Brodie hitting the East River, groped his way to his feet, heard other feet pounding, and tried it the easy way—through the gate he hadn't seen the first time.

He was in a weed-grown back yard with a cracked walk leading to a back porch with sagging screens and a trapezoidal door. He took the steps in a wobbly jump, banged a fist through the rotted wire, raked the hook free from its eyelet and was inside, sniffing a sour odor of decayed wood and imperfectly preserved pears. The door to the interior looked solid; he tried the knob, and it opened. The inside hall was dark, papered in a puce and pale green pattern that was almost invisible under the grease layer. There was a door at the far end under a fanlight that shed a glow like a sunken ship on a strip of worn carpet that hadn't been pretty even when it still had its hair. Just as he reached the big brass knob, a door banged open on his left and a bald-domed gentleman in galluses and armbands flapped a newspaper at him.

"Don't ast," he barked with a rasp like Edison's original recording. "Told you fellers fifty times if I told you once—no use coming around before five pee emm, 'cause she ain't in! And if I hear any more o' that unchristian screeching and hollering you fellers call singing, I'm telephoning Sheriff Hoskins quicker'n Ned Spratt got religion!"

"I'm with you, pop," Blondel reassured him. "I just came to tell you there's a couple of young fellows on the way over to serenade her with steel guitars. They said you were scared to call Hoskins. Said you were picking up KGAS in Peoria on your upper plate. Said you had women in your room, and kept a bottle hidden under the slipcover on the divan. Watch out for 'em. They're tricked out fit to kill in a couple of dandelion-yellow zoot suits, and I'll tell you one more thing," Blondel leaned close enough to get a whiff of Sen-Sen, "they been drinking!"

Blondel got the door open and was out on the sidewalk before his new acquaintance had recovered enough breath to yell "Whippersnapper." There were a few people in sight, looking ordinary enough to be secret agents. Blondel set off at a brisk walk, got as far as the Rexall on the corner before a squad car pulled into sight a block down. He ducked back, heard loud voices, saw a small crowd gathering in front of the house from which he had come. The front door was open, and two tall men in yellow appeared to be having an altercation of some sort with an elderly gentleman wielding a folded newspaper.

There was a neat flush-panel door set in

the imitation stone wall beside Blondel bearing a polished brass panel with names on it. He palmed it open, was in an asbestos tile and plasterboard hall with a menu-board directory of room numbers and names. Tan-carpeted stairs led up. He took them three at a time, whirled around a landing, up more stairs, and was looking out a wide nailed-shut double-hung window at the street below. The squad car was at the curb with the doors hanging open. Down the block, two Monitors were advancing at a brisk stride under the stares of the townsfolk. Blondel ran past closed doors to the far end of the hall, found a dead end, ran back. The sounds of efficient feet were audible now coming up the steps. A door ahead of Blondel opened and a lean woman with wide bony hips stepped out, dragging a lad in a shirt with horizontal stripes—probably a hint of things to come, Blondel judged from the kick the tot swung at his ankle as he slid past into an odor of iodoform and closed the door with his hip. The room was ten feet by twenty. There was a row of hard chairs along one wall, a table with magazines with torn covers, a desk decorated by a wilted rosebud, a couple of ashtrays on stands, a clothes tree bearing a coat and hat. Framed diplomas from a dental college made out to "Rodney H. Maxwell" hung on the pale green wall behind the desk. There was also an inner door, closed and—he tried it—locked. In the hall a shrill female voice seemed to be objecting to something. The feet sounded closer.

Blondel snatched the hat from the rack, slapped it on the back of his head; he tore a strip from an issue of *Time*, with a picture of a ball player who had been dead for three years, wadded it and jammed it into his right cheek; it made a satisfactory bulge. He dropped into the chair and got a magazine open just as the door swung back.

A clean-cut, young America face gave him an interested look, glanced around the room.

"Sir, have you seen anyone enter this room during the last minute or two?" His voice was of the type favored by soap manufacturers.

Blondel gave him a look like a seasick tourist turning down a pork chop.

"You're waiting for the dentist?" the Monitor persisted.

"Wha' ya 'hink, I'm wa'in fer a bus?"

"How long have you been here, sir?" The Monitor came into the room, polite but insistent. His partner was right behind him.

"Who wan's to know? Ge' lost."

"Your name please, sir?"

The locked door behind Blondel opened. He looked up to see a youngish, suntanned face with wavy black hair, a tight line of mouth and heavy-rimmed glasses above starched whites. The newcomer gave the two Monitors an impersonal look, glanced down at Blondel without surprise.

"You can come in now, Mr. Frudlock," he

said and held the door open. Blondel stood, holding his jaw in place with one hand.

"That biscuspid's giving you trouble again, eh, Mr. Frudlock?" The dentist looked solemn. "Maybe we'd better just go ahead with an extraction." Their eyes met; Blondel thought he saw the flicker of an eyelid.

"Wha'ever you say, Doctor, eh, Maxwell." Blondel went past him into a tight little room filled with glass-fronted cases surrounding a chair that made the one at San Quentin look like Granny's rocker. Over the gray-metal bulk of an air conditioner set in the window he could see the street below, with clumps of townfolk gathered here and there to watch the excitement. Only one Monitor was in sight, standing on the corner opposite. Beyond the door he could hear well-modulated voices exchanging highly civilized questions and answers. Then doors clicked and the man in white was sliding inside, looking like a youth who has just set fire to a policeman.

"They're gone," he said, and did something with his right ear.

"Thanks, Doc," Blondel started. The dentist twiddled his ear again. Blondel ignored the eccentricity. "What's the best way out of here?" He motioned to the window. "That route seems a little exposed."

"Who sent you?" The dentist was giving him a one-eyebrow-up look now.

"The yellowjackets chased me in here. They're mad at me because I broke a couple of their toys and then ran out on them. There aren't too many ways to run in your town."

The dentist frowned. "And you just . . . happened along here to my office?"

"That's right."

The dentist moved casually around the table and stationed himself near a filing cabinet. The manner in which his hand hovered near the lock suggested that it contained something besides files.

"Look, Doc," Blondel said hastily. "I don't know what you're thinking, but I'm just a guy who wandered in off the street. I'm grateful to you for shaking those two goons, but now I'll just get on with my paper route." He stepped tward the door.

"Just a minute." The dentist nipped at his lower lip with a tooth that had obviously been brushed twice a day and had seen its dentist twice a year. "What did you do to attract their attention?"

Blondel gave him a brief rundown on his activities. Maxwell smiled when he described the accident to the heli and said "Ah!" when he reached the break from the squad car. "I had a kind of vague idea of making it to some town they haven't hit yet," Blondel concluded. "But it looks like they planned this thing right down to the cheese in the mousetrap."

The dentist nodded. "All right, I'll take a chance on you," he said crisply. "You may be a plant, but if you are, you'll live to

regret it—just barely." He turned and opened
a drawer marked KIL-KUR, twiddled things,
and slipped out a soft-leather holster with a
small shiny gun with a long slim barrel. It
disappeared under his left arm. "Come on."
Blondel followed him into the outer office;
Maxwell paused long enough to make a minute adjustment to the angle at which his
second-best diploma hung, then eased open
the door and slid out. They went along the
hall, in through a door, just like the others,
that concealed a narrow stair that led down
to a fire door opening on a parking lot occupied by three nondescript sedans and a pearl-
gray custom-bodied Mercedes 300 SL. Maxwell slid behind the wheel of the latter, and
Blondel climbed in the other side in a heady
perfume of glove leather and waxed inlay
work. The door closed with a click like a
watchcase.

"Where are we going?" Blondel inquired.

"My place," Maxwell said shortly and dug
off with a soft *rhoom!* like a secret weapon
leaving the launching pad. A block up the
street they passed a gold-striped Monitors'
car parked in a gas station. Nobody appeared to notice them, except an expen-
sively corseted middle-aged matron who
gave Maxwell a wave and a smile that suggested that Doc had that first million made,
if he stuck around town long enough to
collect it.

*   *   *

It was a breezy ten-mile drive north along the kind of winding, tree-hung road that suggested picnic baskets in the rumble seats of Model A Fords. They made it in nine minutes by the dash clock, topped a rise, and saw a spread of neatly-tended acreage with a brick and glass house that could have been lifted from any professional-class suburban street in the country. Blondel could see a long graveled drive leading up a slope of lawn past a stretch of wall behind which a stray shaft of late sun struck a patch of yellow.

He grabbed the wheel, hauled it back as Maxwell swung out to turn in.

"Gun it!"

Maxwell's reactions were quick; he straightened the Mercedes out with no more than a little slithering of loose shoulder-gravel and booted her hard.

"It was a stake-out," Blondel yelled over the roar of the wind. "Unless you've got a houseboy who wears yellow."

Maxwell's eyes went to the rear-view minor; they tightened at the corners. He said something under his breath. Blondel looked back. The garage door was up and a police car was just poking its snout out; a yellow-clad figure was running toward it from the house.

"I wonder how . . ." Maxwell cut his eyes at Blondel.

"They traced me to your office," he said, "and called for the ambush as soon as they found you gone. Keep your eyes on the road. I'm not going to jump—in either direction." The little car howled around a curve posted 35, straightened out in time to enter another. Maxwell was staring straight ahead, his lips parted, eyes bright. "Fasten your belt," he said. "This may be a little hectic.

"You think you can outrun them?"

"I may not be faster—but I know the roads."

"They've got helis."

Maxwell glanced at the sun, just above treetop level now. "I have a few tricks, too." His tone suggested that he was pretty well satisfied with the way things were going.

"For a quiet little hometown dentist you're full of surprises, Doc."

"Not all of us were as somnolent as the enemy imagined," Maxwell said. "We knew this day was coming. We're not entirely unprepared."

"Who's *'we'*?"

Maxwell ignored the question, drifted the SL around another ungraded turn, kicked out of it, went away wide open, did what the British call a racing change through a wobbly S curve that had been designed to save a tree that had quite probably been a sapling when Pocahontas was selling trade goods to John Smith. Blondel got a flash of the Interceptor just coming into the straightaway half a mile behind.

"They're gaining," he said.

"Open the top boot." Maxwell nodded at

the black mohair cover buttoned down behind them with big chrome snaps. Blondel
lifted a corner; Maxwell poked something
on the dash and a panel slid back, exposing
the gleaming walnut butt of a rifle nestled
down under the parcel tray. Blondel looked
at him and shook his head. Maxwell turned
the corners of his mouth down.

"This isn't a game of cops and robbers,"
he barked. "It's war!"

"So far, all they've got on me is resisting
arrest, grand larceny, and assault and battery," Blondel called over the racket of the
slipstreams. "I believe I'll pass up the murder rap, if it's all the same to you."

"Start facing realities!" Maxwell twisted
the wheel hard, slithered fifty yards on two
wheels, straightened out without a pause in
the flow of his rhetoric. "Principles don't
exist in a vacuum. If you believe in a thing
you either fight for it, or stand by and watch
it die."

"I'm not sure killing people is exactly
what my principles have in mind," Blondel
protested.

"Scruples are fine—if you live to use them!
Survival comes first!"

"Yeah—but me minus my scruples is just
a hundred and eighty pounds of unsatisfied
appetites for all the wrong things."

"Dead appetites—unless you're willing to
stand up for what you believe!"

"What I believe seems to vary. Right now

I believe I won't shoot at those boys unless they shoot first."

"Very well." Maxwell was watching the rear-view alertly. "Anything to be obliging ..." There was a gentle curve coming up ahead, lined with amber-leaved trees silhouetted against a meadow that sloped up to a stand of second-growth oak. Maxwell swung wide—too wide. The right wheels chopped underbrush. Blondel winced at the sound of untrimmed jimson weed whipping at the paint job. Behind them the pursuit car was coming up fast, attempting to close. The curve tightened; Maxwell fought the Mercedes, still watching the mirror. They were in a skid, howling along at a forty-five degree angle to the direction of travel. Ahead, heavy sawhorses stood across the road before a raw slash of dug-up pavement between big trees. Blondel braced himself for the imminent crash—

Maxwell hit the gas pedal and the SL veered, leaped straight for the dense undergrowth to the left of the road. Blondel ducked as the car bounced hard, raking her bottom, and shot between thick trunks, crashed through brush, bucking up a ragged rise to burst out in the clear on a potholed and weed-grown single lane road. The screech of its brakes mingled with a similar howl behind. Blondel winced at the smash that came then, followed by crashing sounds, metallic pings, a crackling. He let out a long breath.

"You're a fast man back of a wheel, Maxwell." The dentist looked smug.

"Week-end rally driving has its uses," he said.

Blondel opened his door. "Let's go down and take a look."

"Never mind that." Maxwell backed the Mercedes, preparing to drive on. Blondel stepped out, headed for the rough path the car had cut, without waiting to see whether the other followed.

He emerged on the road below, fifty feet from where the police car lay on its side beyond what was left of the barricade, its front wheels angled hard left and spinning out of round. Dusky orange flames were licking up around the twisted front bumper. Maxwell came up behind Blondel. "Looks as though they missed the turn," he said in a tone as elaborately casual as a pool hustler's. "Now let's get out of here—"

"They're still in there!" Through the starred windshield one of the Monitors was groping at the door above him. A quick ripple of fire ran back along the underside of the car, leaped high with a *whoof!* when it hit puddled gas under the tank. Blondel sprinted for it, came around on the upwind side, reached in over the dented top for the door handle. It was wedged tight. He scrambled up on top of the wreck, tried again; it was jammed as solid as the main vault door at Fort Knox.

"Come on, you fool!" Maxwell yelled.

Blondel tried the rear door. The frame was twisted out of line. He stamped smashed glass from the rear frame, reached down for a grip on a slack arm, hauled hard. The Monitor, he discovered, was heavier than he looked—a good two hundred pounds, as limp as a wet sail. The fire was booming up behind Blondel now; paint crackled like hot fat.

". . . a car," Maxwell shouted. "Leave them and come on!"

Blondel got a grip under the Monitor's arms and heaved him out on the side. There was a snarl of a double-clutched engine, then a *skreel* of brakes and a second police car shot into view, pushing a spray of dust beside it. It rocked to a stop half through the broken barricade and the doors popped wide. Maxwell whirled and disappeared into the brush. Four tall, long-legged men in yellow came pelting up toward the burning car. Blondel shoved the man he had gotten out down across the side of the car.

"Jump, sir!" one of the Monitors called, and a gust whirled fire around the seat of Blondel's pants. He jumped. Two Monitors closed in on him, held him up while he coughed smoke and knuckled pain tears into his eyeballs. He looked back and saw two men on top of the car, passing down the second man. Then they were all running. In the distance Blondel caught the roar of Maxwell's SL gunning up to speed just as the tank blew. Fire fountained over half an acre of woods. Three of the Monitors went trotting off, efficiently aiming little gadgets like pen-cell flashlights at the blazes. The one who was still holding Blondel's arm cleared his throat as deferentially as a waiter presenting a padded bar bill.

"Sir, I must ask you to go with us back to the village."

The other Monitors were coming back now. They ringed Blondel in. Their manner, while not precisely ominous, invited no liberties.

"Sure," Blondel said wearily. "I guess we were bound to get together sooner or later."

CHAPTER THREE

It was a silent ride back into town. Blondel assayed a question or two which netted him courteous but uninformative replies. The car made a brief stop at the police station, which seemed to be full of Monitors, with a few city cops and state troopers standing around outside looking puffy and unhealthy next to the trim figures in yellow. Then they drove on through town and down a bumpy dirt road to a small grass-strip airport. There was a gold heli waiting, similar to the one Blondel had rammed earlier. Two Monitors escorted him to it, got in with him. The machine lifted, hummed along at treetop level for a few miles, then circled and settled in on a wide lawn that looked black in the deep twilight, except where floodlights made green pools. Blondel climbed out and stared at the big, bright-lit gray stone house with gabled roofs, chimneys, a porte-cochere, and long low outbuildings behind.

The Monitors escorted him up wide steps between potted *arbor vitaes* into a high-ceilinged hall with polished ash flooring showing around pink and gold Persian rugs. There were shiny, spindle-legged tables, a big gilt-framed mirror, a painting of an old pirate in mutton chops.

There was a short wait, then a polite Monitor ushered him along to a big white-painted oak door standing invitingly half open. He stepped through it into a library that looked half the size of the one at Yale.

Across the room a small, fatherly-looking old gentleman, in a loose toga-like garment sat behind a big rosewood desk beside a tier of books that was lost in shadows at the top. Through a wide, curtained window behind him Blondel could see a stretch of flood-lit lawn. There was an expensive odor of hand-rolled cigars and tooled bindings and the kind of furniture wax which is applied by hand at body heat according to a formula known only to a secret guild of elves. Blondel shifted from one foot to the other, and wondered what Maxwell was doing now.

"Tell me frankly," the old genleman leaned forward and gave him a look that invited confidence, "why you felt it necessary to run away." He had a voice like the "amen" notes on an electric organ.

"Well—after all, I, ah, didn't know who you fellows were," Blondel extemporized.

The old man said, "Ah," and nodded as though he had found the explanation quite enlightening. "Of course. Well, we shall quickly set that aright. I am the Tersh Jetterax." His tone indicated that he had just cleared up a weighty mystery. "I have been assigned the responsibility for the well-being of all citizens in this zone," he added, with a smile like a good-natured professor rebuking his star pupil for missing an easy one. "Your help will make my task easier."

"Why should I want to make your task easier?" Blondel demanded.

"Why not?" The Tersh Jetterax smiled disarmingly.

"Well—you *did* invade the country," Blondel reminded him.

"Ummm. An unfortunate turn of phrase. Why don't you just think of us as kindly visitors?"

"Kindly visitors don't usually kick out the cops and take over," Blondel pointed out.

"You resent our replacement of your police forces?" The Tersh looked astonished. "But they were inefficient, inadequate, unjust—"

"Still, they were *my* cops, not out-of-town slickers with gas guns that turn healthy Irish tempers into vacant looks!"

"*Your* cops? Really, Mr. Blondel—how much did you, personally, actually have to do with the administration of police regulations, the appointment of police officers, even with the formulation of the laws they were charged to enforce?"

"Well, I had the right to vote for the legislators—or whoever it is that decides to install parking meters and No Left Turn signs. . . ."

"Ummm. The Police Commission. And who appoints them?"

"Beats me," Blondel admitted. "But—"

"Be candid, Mr. Blondel. Can you in conscience support a system which levies arrest quotas on uneducated and underpaid factota who busy themselves by subjecting you to embarrassment, inconvenience, discourtesy, detention and twenty-dollar fines for merely slowing to two miles per hour instead of coming to a full stop when crossing a deserted intersection—an intersection built with your tax money—while the theft of your bicycle or the rifling of your home by burglars goes uncorrected, nine times out of ten?"

"Not exactly, but—"

"We have merely replaced an ineffective system with a just and efficient one; an imperfect government with one totally dedicated to your welfare," the Tersh spelled out placidly. "Now you can turn your attention to self-development, secure in the knowledge that your society will not capriciously penalize you for the enrichment or aggrandizement of inept or venal bureaucrats."

"If you don't mind my asking—why bother to convince me? You've caught me. What happens now?"

"Mr. Blondel, you are the first of your fellow citizens I've had the pleasure of talking to, face to face. Your apparent unwillingness to co-operate with your new government is a cause of deep concern to me."

"I didn't co-operate too well with the old one. I wouldn't hold out much hope for any improvement."

The Tersh spread his hands and showed an Honest-Bewilderment look. "My government will conduct your affairs in accordance with the highest principles of your own ethical systems."

"Thanks—but the fact is, we prefer to conduct our own affairs in accordance with whatever principles strike our fancies."

"This intense loyalty you apparently feel— to what is it actually attached, Mr. Blondel?" The old man looked at him as though he suspected him of holding out on the secret of the Universe. "Is it the countryside, the hills and trees? If so, rest assured we plan no major topographical modifications. Is it the fluctuating roster of persons who comprise the national population? They will continue to thrive and, in fact, will find their lot vastly improved. Is it the documents on which your previous regime was nominally based? Let me put your mind at rest: Our rule will be based on this same Constitution, more faithfully interpreted than by your own elected officials."

"But at least they *were* elected," Blondel reminded him.

"Your childlike confidence in the persons who count the votes astonishes me." The Tersh smiled sympathetically. "And the nominees—they were your personal choices?"

"Maybe I wouldn't have picked the exact candidates," Blondel hedged, "but—"

"Mr. Blondel, do you actually have any knowledge of how these high matters were conducted? Did you participate, even by proxy, in the last-minute closed-door convention sessions in which deals were made before the final ballot? Do you know what the demonstrated policies of the participants were, their voting records, their private interests, their political indebtednesses?"

"Confidentially, politics always kind of bored me," Blondel said.

The old gentleman gave Blondel a long sad look, and heaved a patient-sounding sigh. He may or may not have twiddled something under the edge of the desk; the door opened behind Blondel. Two good-looking young men in yellow came in, as crisp and snappy as something one obtained by sending in cereal boxtops.

"Mr. Blondel," the Tersh said, sounding a little grieved, "I would like very much for you to participate in the short indoctrination course which I've set up to explain our mission here to, ah, dissenters like yourself.

I cannot, of course, *insist* on your co-operation—but I ask you, as one bearer of good will to another, to grant me this request."

"Have I got any choice?"

"Perhaps if you merely looked upon this as an opportunity to learn more about us . . ."

There was a pause during which Blondel's imagination ran through a number of potential alternatives.

"Well," he said. "As long as I'm here—why not?"

"Excellent!" The Tersh beamed. "And we will talk again in a few days."

Blondel rose; the Monitors closed in.

"Ah—one other thing . . ." the Tersh said.

Blondel turned back.

"In view of your, ah, attitudes, Mr. Blondel—why did you risk your life to save two of my Monitors?"

Blondel lifted his shoulders in a vague shrug. The Tersh was looking baffled as Blondel went out into the hall.

Blondel's escort led him up a wide, white-bannistered, red-carpeted staircase and along a wallpapered hall to a big white door with a gold knob, standing ajar. Inside there were rugs, a desk, bookcases, an easy chair, a table and lamp, a four-poster, an inner door leading to a tile bath, and a pair of windows with airy curtains and heavy lined drapes, looking out on the lawn as exposed as a billiard table under the lights.

The Monitors left with wishes for a nice sleep. Blondel tried to close the door. It stuck tight, standing open an inch. The room was less private than it appeared.

He tried out the shower, used a pair of purple-and-yellow striped pajamas from the bureau drawer, crawled in between heavy linen sheets. He went to sleep pondering the problem of what the Tersh Jetterax hoped to accomplish by treating him like visiting royalty.

Blondel rose late the next morning. Downstairs, a dried-up little man in old-fashioned butler's livery and a Hotel-Splendide manner drew out a chair and offered ham and eggs Stroganoff. He was on his second cup of hand-brewed coffee when a Monitor came in and conveyed an invitation to meet someone in the conservatory.

The latter turned out to be a cheery glassed-in porch with tanks of fish, potted plants, bird cages, and high-backed wicker chairs in one of which a long-legged, pipe-smoking individual in a tweed jacket and a toothbrush mustache was sitting relaxed. He puffed out blue smoke with an odor of cookies baking, and waved Blondel toward a chair next to a gray sphere like a metal beach ball mounted on a stand.

"Good morning, Mr. Blondel," he called, full of early-morning cheer. "Sleep well?"

"I've already had the opening lecture," Blondel told him. "Maybe we could save time if you'll just skip ahead to the 'consequences'?"

The man's bushy salt-and-pepper eyebrows

went up to meet his bushy salt-and-pepper
hairline.

"Mr. Blondel," his smile had stiffened a
trifle, "please let your fancy rest. We are
precisely what the Tersh Jetterax has already told you—well-wishers to you and
your people. My name is Frokinil, and I
hope we'll become good friends."

Blondel sat down gingerly. "What do *you*
get out of all this?"

"The satisfaction of doing our duty."

"I mean, you, personally. What's your
payoff? The High Command going to set
you up as Duke of Brooklyn, or King of
New Jersey?"

"You're talking nonsense, Mr. Blondel."
The grin was definitely glassy now. "I'm
here to oversee the testing program for the
zone, and devise appropriate skill-distri-
butions manifolds."

"Slave labor camps, eh?"

Frokinil *tsk!*ed impatiently. "Mr. Blondel,
can't you rid your mind of these grotesque
stereotypes? Surely you're too rational a
man to be governed by mystical allegiances
to symbols that are violated daily, publicly,
without so much as a blush!"

"Frankly, the sight of you fellows walking
around on our real estate without a pass-
port seems to arouse some instincts I didn't
know I had."

Frokinil leaned forward, preparing for a
cozy intellectual discussion. "Very well. To
recognize one's own bias is the beginning of

insight. You act from an instinctive impulse to perpetuate a regime which has the sanction of tribal tradition." He stood briskly and motioned to the metal globe on the stand.

"Just step here a moment, Mr. Blondel, if you will. I'd like you to consider some facts." Blondel complied.

"Consider your typical elementary school . . ." Frokinil flicked his fingers at the machine and its surface glazed, became milky; a dazzling glow sprang up from it. Blondel blinked and suddenly was standing just inside the door of what was obviously an elementary school room, with cut-outs of witches and pumpkins pasted on the windows, and rows of children with faces as bright as toy lanterns sitting with their hands folded, chanting raggedly together:

". . . one-nation-inavisable-with-liberty-and-justice-for-all."

"All right, you, Walter. I got my eye on you," a lumpy-bodied little woman with an untidy bun of gray hair said in a voice like a shutter on a haunted house. "You just set quiet today, or you'll be back down to Mr. Funder's office quicker'n a nigger'll steal whiskey."

A small boy hung his head and glanced sideways, left-right.

"All right, now." The woman thumbed a bra strap back in place and yanked down a wall map. "Get out yer jogerfy books and turn to page nineteen." She picked up a pointer and peered at the big colored map of the United States; her lips moved silently. The kids thumped books, flipped pages, fired a couple of fast paper wads. The lady turned and stabbed with the pointer.

"Lucilla, tell 'em the names of the capitals of the states." A small girl with tight braids promptly chirped: "Muntgum, Reefeenix, L'il Rock . . ."

"This prototype of wisdom and aesthetics is placed before these impressionable young minds and charged with the duty of drilling them in rotes." Frokinil's voice came out of the air by Blondel's right ear. "The only useful training being acquired here is some small skill in ballistics."

The schoolroom faded into a misty glow that changed shape like smoke cloud and congealed into a wide, airy stretch of green grass under big trees. Groups of half a dozen or so children were scattered across the park, each accompanied by an adult in a toga. Some of them seemed to be examining the bark of trees, or clumps of leaves on low branches; others were kneeling, poking in the earth. One group was gathered around a table, fiddling with glass retorts and tubes.

"Under the new order," Frokinil said, "teachers who have devoted their lives to training for the practice of this vital profession work to instill an understanding of the realities of nature and art as the basis for true wisdom . . ."

"Sounds tougher than the three R's,"

Blondel contributed. "But will it pay union scale?"

". . . Of course," Frokinil was ploughing on, "not all human minds are fully functional. There will be many tasks for which mental defectives are suited . . ."

The sunny lawn whiffed out of sight, and Blondel was blinking at a long bare room where a row of slack-faced youngsters in loose white garments like flour-bag night-gowns sat on stools bleating and flapping their arms at a camera. A flashbulb washed the walls with blue-white; one of the in-mates fell off his stool. A grim-looking old woman in stiff grays yanked him up and jerked him back in line.

"Your institutions for these unfortunates are little more than zoos," Frokinil stated. "Those few capable of absorbing the skills of table waiting or fruit picking are released on society to make their own way, to breed freely, reinfecting the stock with their defective genes. Under the new system, they will receive appropriate training, and will live carefully-controlled and supervised lives—without the opportunity of propagating their tragedies."

"Kind of tough on the free idiots of the world," Blondel noted.

"Consider the care given the indigent normal under the old system," Frokinil bored on. The gloomy institutional scene faded and they were standing by a long desk under a sign that said ADMISSIONS. A thin little woman with a caved-in face and a paper corsage was shaking her head at a big, stolid-looking fellow with swarthy skin and an acne-scarred face. He was supporting a barrel-shaped woman with one arm. Her head lolled against his shoulder. A clock on the wall showed two A.M.

". . . owe the hospital for the *last* confinement, Mr. Orosco," the sharp-faced woman was saying. "If you can't make advance payment, you'll have to take her elsewhere."

"You goddam crazy, woman!" the man yelled. "Rachel's gonna have the baby right now, maybe in one minute! Where's a doctor?" He slammed a fist down on the counter-top. "I gotta have a doctor for Rachel, I got to have him now, son of a bitch . . . where's a doctor!"

The little woman whirled to a side door back of the counter and met a husky young attendant coming in.

"He's cursing me, Timmy! The damn wetback—"

The swarthy man was moving toward a door marked NO ADMITTANCE, dragging the woman with him. He was swearing loudly in Spanish. The attendant ran to intercept him. They grappled, and the woman fell. The man stooped to her, and the attendant set himself and hit him a terrific blow back of the ear. He went to his hands and knees—

Blondel took a step and a hand caught his arm. The scene faded and dissolved into bright mist.

"Calmly, Mr. Blondel," Frokinil chided. "This is merely a recording, you know."

"You're nuts," Blondel said. "Nothing like that happens in our hospitals. Doctors take an oath—"

"This scene, or variations of it, takes place hundreds of times every day in virtually every hospital on the continent. Not only are the sick and injured turned away if they fail to show adequate financial resources, but malpractice—and I use the term within the context of your own, present-day medical knowledge—accounts for approximately thirty deaths per day, while hospital-acquired infections account for a further—"

"OK, the hospitals are overloaded; but we're building more."

"Not as rapidly as the population is increasing. Few public facilities are keeping pace with births. And yet no control whatever is exercised over the latter."

"There'll be legislation on that in a few more years—"

"You don't have a few more years, Mr. Blondel. And it would have been a very long time before a fully effective program would have been initiated. Meanwhile, your slums were proliferating . . ."

Blondel grabbed for support; he seemed to be floating in mid-air, looking down on a narrow, grimy street festooned with fire escapes and clotheslines. ". . . your courts' backlogs increase . . ." The slum street dissolved into an old-fashioned, high-ceilinged room packed with spectators, lawyers, bailiffs, cops, bondsmen, defendants, and relatives. A querulous-looking judge perched on the bench, shuffling papers; his mouth twitched as though he was needing a drink bad.

"Remanded to custody," he barked. "I'm setting the hearing for . . ." he shuffled more papers. "I'll set the date later, Harry," he said to a shifty-eyed fellow in a chalk-stripe, who nodded. A lanky man with a hangdog look grabbed his arm.

"Hey, I got a job to hold down . . ." The sharpie shook him off. The judge banged his gavel. The defendant was still talking as the guard hustled him away.

". . . and so long as your legal profession was designed primarily to generate legal fees, the trend would never have been reversed," Frokinil was saying blandly. "The situation is no better with regard to higher education, care of orphans, treatment of unwed mothers, the aged and the infirm, minority groups, criminals—" Grim scenes formed and faded like documentary D.T.'s. "Do you mean me to believe, Mr. Blondel," Frokinil concluded in a gently reproving tone, "that all these abuses meet with your full approval?"

"Why don't you stick to invading the country and skip the complaints?" Blondel proposed. "If you don't like it you can go back where you came from and let us handle it our own way."

"What is your own way? Do you ever question the programs you read of in your favorite picture-magazine, or even gain a true understanding of what they entail? Have you any personal knowledge of the laws relating to the insane, divorce, rape, insurance, marriage, suicide, pure food, bankruptcy, misleading advertising, fraud, citizen arrest, kidnapping, assault and battery, sodomy, witchcraft—"

"What do you mean—witchcraft? We haven't believed in that since the 1600's!"

"You're wrong, Mr. Blondel. Witchcraft is a punishable offense in parts of this zone today. What about the laws governing use of liquor and narcotics, smuggling, bearing arms—"

"I've got you on that one," Blondel cut him off. "It says right in the Constitution that the right to bear arms shall not be abridged."

"Your right to bear arms has been sharply abridged, Mr. Blondel, and not without reason. There are also a number of curious laws dealing with vagrancy, loitering, trespass, zoning, et cetera; all affecting your personal liberty, with which every citizen would do well to familiarize himself—but the complexity of the codes makes that impossible, of course, even if the desire were there, which it isn't. We have changed all that. The new laws are rational, enforceable and just, and will apply with absolute impartiality to every citizen. There will be no more bribes, graft, lobby pressure...."

Frokinil swam into view as the fog dissipated to reveal the fish-tanks and potted plants of the conservatory, and the little gray sphere that had projected the pictures.

"You don't get the idea," Blondel told him. "We Americans aren't a bunch of Pavlov's pet poodles, standing around waiting for a signal to get hungry. In this country—"

"—your opinions are moulded by an irresponsible press which feeds on advertising accounts and state department handouts designed to whitewash the latter. You travel as you like—provided you've paid the appropriate taxes, passed the required inspections, have adequate funds, and have no personal enemies on the police forces. You eat whatever suits your tastes—if you can pay for it; you spend your time as you wish—with the permission of your employer—"

"I'm a free-lance pilot. If I don't like my job, I can move on."

"You're fortunate. But still—you need *some* job. And when your unregulated economy produces another depression, you might find your keen sense of personal determination yielding to the need for food and a warm bed."

"OK, maybe it isn't Utopia—but we like doing it our own way . . . without any help from a blimp-load of foreigners!"

"Mr. Blondel . . ." Frokinil put a perfectly groomed hand on Blondel's arm. "Think of the welfare of your children—of future generations! Your petty nationalisms of to-day will mean no more to them than Queen Boadicea does to you!"

"My ancestors were on the other side."

"You're simply adopting a stance." Frok-inil was beginning to look exasperated. "You're not opening your mind to what we're trying to show you! We offer you, at last, what you've always dreamed of but never expected—perfect government, and you reject it because it did not spring, miraculously, from those same imperfect functionaries who have victimized you over the years!"

"I had the same chance as anyone else to be head man," Blondel pointed out. "I just never went in for politics."

"Politics—by which you mean a semifor-malized system for determining who will exploit the substratum; a closed in-group of the initiated making a business of looting the common wealth—"

"That Socialist jargon gives me the sleep-ies, Mr. Frokinil," Blondel advised him.

"Can't I make you see it?" Frokinil frowned.

"Maybe I'm just too dumb to make a down payment on a bargain in gold bricks," Blondel suggested. Frokinil flapped his arms.

"Here are you, a native of a world wealthy enough to fulfill your every material require-ment, member of a race biologically ad-vanced enough to provide every intellectual and aesthetic satisfaction. Yet you live in uncertainty, emotional impoverishment, even physical need, your own potentialities unexplored and unfulfilled." Frokinil waved a hand in an expansive gesture. "What we offer you is the inheritance due you, your innate right as a man to enjoy the best fruits of existence."

"I've already got more rights than I know what to do with," Blondel protested. "Just turn me loose and I'll get on with what I was doing. As it happens, I've got a lead on a job in Ecuador—"

"Poof!—I'm not referring to rewarding indolence with official doles or the legislation of artificial social states. I'm speaking of making use of your potentialities!"

"What potentialities?"

"Can you walk a tightrope, Mr. Blondel?"

"No—but—"

"Can you play the piano, the violin, the oboe? Can you fence, juggle, carry out a qualitative analysis, identify birdcalls, practice judo, medicine, or law? Can you type, ride a unicycle, deal from the bottom of a deck, paint, sculpt, apply a proper finish to wood? Have you knowledge of ceramics, bookbinding, pole vaulting, mountain climbing—"

"No, but I can fly that airplane," Blondel got in.

Frokinil nodded, smiling his saddest smile. "So you can, Mr. Blondel, so you can." For some reason, that seemed to end the conversation.

Later that afternoon, in a small classroom

fitted with elaborate visual aids, Blondel dozed fitfully as Frokinil lectured persuasively on the beauties of the new regime:

"It's what you've always wanted: wise, honest government," the invader concluded. "So won't you join in now, and help rather than hinder the Liberation?"

"Howzzat?" Blondel came to with a start. "Oh, are you still here?"

"Mr. Blondel!" Frokinil wailed. "I don't think you're really *trying* to be fair!"

Blondel rose and stretched. "You just don't get the idea, Frocky," he said. "Look at it this way. . . ." He went to the blackboard, chalked two dots a foot apart.

"This is you Monitors," he indicated one dot. "This is me, over here." He pointed to the other. "You can wipe me out." He erased his dot with a swipe of his hand. "But you can't move me over to your dot." He scribed a circle around the latter. "That's your dot, and you're in it all alone. . . ." He broke off at the look on Frokinil's face. The instructor was gripping the back of a chair; his eyes were squeezed shut.

"Take . . . take it away," he said in a choked voice.

Blondel looked around. "Take what away?"

"That . . . that diagram. Erase it—please— quickly!"

Puzzled, Blondel complied.

"OK, it's gone. You can come out now."

Frokinil opened one eye. He sighed hugely and almost fell into a chair.

"What was that all about?"

"Just . . . a momentary dizziness."

"Dizziness my left patella! What was there about a few lines on a blackboard that would make a smoothie like you stage a flipout?"

"Well, as a matter of fact—it was the . . . the circle around the symbolic representation of . . . of ourselves."

"Huh?"

"A small eccentricity." Frokinil managed a pale smile. "Just as you, perhaps, have an irrational fear of heights, so we suffer from what our scientists term 'fear of closure'; it has its roots in our early evolutionary history when we were small, burrowing animals."

"I never knew you Bolsheviks considered yourselves supermoles," Blondel said. "I suppose that's Lysenko's latest noncapitalist theory."

"I've told you repeatedly—but never mind." Frokinil stood, still pale. "I'd appreciate it if you'd keep this little incident confidential. Rather embarrassing, you know—"

"And *that's* why most of the doors in this fancy jail don't close," Blondel said.

"Please—let's just leave this our little secret," Frokinil appealed. "Just consider it evidence that, after all, we too have our little, er, human failings."

"It's evidence of something," Blondel agreed. "I'm not sure what."

CHAPTER FOUR

At dinner that evening, Frokinil introduced two fellow guests to Blondel. One was a small, round-shouldered youth with untrimmed hair and fingernails, who ate his soup with sound effects and didn't talk. His name was Pleech. The other was a tall, ruddy-faced, hearty fellow, introduced as Aunderson, who wore three lodge buttons on his lapel. An expanse of expensive wrist watch and cuff showed when he peeled his cigar.

As soon as the last of the Monitors had trailed Frokinil from the room, Aunderson leaned toward Blondel. "What do you think of the layout?" He shot the question from the side of his mouth.

"They feed OK," he replied cautiously.

Aunderson hitched his chair closer. "They're

careless," he hissed. "Overconfident. They leave doors open."

"So?"

He shot Blondel a sharp look, like a man listening to criticism of mother's cooking. "Brother, don't you want to get away from here?"

"I hadn't thought much about it."

Aunderson drew on the cigar and looked at Blondel sideways. "By God, now I've heard everything," he stated.

"They don't leave doors open by accident, man," Pleech said in a breathy tone. "They're eyeballing every move."

The big fellow hitched his chair away from Blondel, flicked his eyes at the corners of the room. "Place is probably bugged," he muttered. He patted his pockets, brought out a ball-point and a business card; he cupped the card in his hand and jotted on it, passed it to Blondel below table-top level.

"THE KID'S A FINK. DROP BY MY ROOM AF-TER DARK."

Blondel sighed and tucked the card away. The trio finished the meal in silence.

Back in his room, Blondel sat in the big soft chair and listened to the small sounds going on elsewhere in the house, remembering the previous afternoon: the big gold blimps, floating down; the crack troops in their yellow suits, and the blaring voices coming on over every loud-speaker in the city, announcing that the invaders had arrived.

He got up and took a turn up and down the room. So far, the pattern had failed to fit Blondel's preconceived notions of how an invasion should be managed. Where were the dive bombers and the big guns and the paratroopers and the tanks rumbling in through the rubble? What were the Air Force and the Army doing against the enemy? How much territory had been taken over? Had the Pentagon hit back with the nuclear strike force or the Polaris fleet? His right hand twitched in a reflex urge to turn on a television set and get the Word.

There was a soft footfall outside and Aunderson poked his face around the door, frowned at all four corners of the room, then slid inside.

"Well, what do you think?" he whispered.

"Slim was right," Blondel said. "They leave the doors open on purpose."

"Yes." Aunderson tipped his head toward the one he had just come through. "Jammed open. They're watching, all right."

"And listening."

The visitor clamped his jaw shut, prowled the room looking under things, then sat on the edge of the bed and jiggled a foot. Blondel waited. Outside a light wind made a sighing sound in the branches of a tree.

"What do you think of their story?" Aunderson muttered suddenly. He gave the appearance of trying to talk without moving his lips.

"Sounds good," Blondel said. Aunderson's

head jerked. "Too good," Blondel added. Aunderson relaxed.

"You . . . ah . . . have any plans?" Aunderson watched the toe of his shoe.

"I plan to rub GI soap in my armpit," Blondel said from the side of his mouth. "I'll run a fever; when they take me away to the hospital I'll steal a jug of medicinal brandy and shack up in a broom closet with a redheaded nurse until they go away."

Aunderson's head jerked again. "This is no time for boffs, fellow," he said sternly. "What kind of American are you?"

"I tear up traffic tickets and chisel on my income tax right along with the rest of you," Blondel reassured him. "I'm no scab."

"Just after dinner would be the best time," Aunderson said. "They overeat. Makes 'em sluggish."

"Yeah?"

"Absolutely."

"Tonight would be better." Blondel was not moving his lips either.

"Eh?"

"While they're asleep."

Aunderson hitched a little closer, listening intently for the details. "Go on, fellow."

"That's all," Blondel said. "Don't play dumb. Go back to your room and stand by. I'll let you know."

Aunderson stood up. "Any, ah, preparations I ought to make?"

"Naturally. Tear all your sheets into two-inch strips. Better go into the john to do it.

If they see you they might catch wise. Work quietly and keep your lips buttoned."

"The door won't close." Aunderson blushed a little.

"Get behind it."

"And knot them together?"

"Not unless your lips are a lot looser than mine."

"I mean the sheets."

"Naturally. Don't waste my time with routine questions. I assume your inoculations are in order?"

"What's that? You mean cholera, typhoid, and so on?"

"I don't mean hiccups."

"As it happens, Myrtle and I took a South American cruise just last fall. I think I've got them all."

"That's it, then. And check all suspicious sounds, odors, and moving lights."

"Right." He stood. Halfway through the door he turned back. "Who are you with? FBI? CIA? SOS?"

"KGGF."

"That's a radio station."

"Sure—do I have to spell it out for you?"

"Sorry. They, ah, in touch with you?"

"You didn't think all those pigeons outside were wild, did you?"

"What pigeons? I didn't see any pigeons."

"That's the idea; deny everything. Better get going now. A lot to do before midnight."

He nodded and went away. Blondel

stretched out on the bed and wondered about some of the people on Our Side.

Ten minutes later a board creaked. Blondel sat up, expecting to see Frokinil appear, full of optimism and statistics. Nothing happened. Blondel rose and went to the door, put his head out. Aunderson was just disappearing down the stairs, carrying a pair of highly-polished Scotch grain brogans under his arm. Blondel stepped out and went along to the head of the stairs, saw Aunderson go through an archway down below. He listened for a few seconds, then went down after him. The arch led into a small dark room; Blondel picked his way over mops and brooms, came out in a papered hall. He could hear voices off to the left. The door they were coming from was open an inch or so.

". . . tearing sheets into strips." Aunderson was saying. "And—"

"But, my dear sir, it's not at all necessary for you to barter for special consideration!" The Tersh Jetterax sounded upset. "I assure you, after your testing is complete, you'll each be recommended for appropriate training—"

"Look here, I'm not some kind of farmer or manual laborer." Aunderson sounded indignant. "I can face facts; I know which way the wind's blowing. I saw those big yellow airships and—"

"Please, sir! I appreciate your advising

me of poor Mr. Blondel's misguided plans, but there is nothing I could promise you that you will not receive freely, as a gift due you as a member of the human race!"

"Now, look! I may be a prisoner of war— well, hell yes, your boys nailed me fair and square, I concede that—but a man like me can be a big *help* to you—"

"Mr. Aunderson, it is *you* I wish to help! Of course, in the case of Mr. Blondel, I see that it will be necessary to use more, ah, direct measures to establish a true personality-rapport; but this is only in his own interest, of course."

"Uh—you're not figuring on messing around with *my* personality?" Aunderson sounded worried now.

"I do hope that won't be necessary. . . ."

Blondel faded back along the hall, inspired by a sudden urge to put distance between the kindly Tersh's personality alterers and himself. While his ego wasn't much, he conceded, it was the one he had come in with and he had a lively desire to keep it the way it was, flaws and all.

Around the first corner, light shone from a half-open door. Blondel peeked inside. The bearded youth from the dinner table was standing by a bookcase with a folio-size volume in his hands. He looked up and saw Blondel.

"The wildest, man." He hefted the book. "Like it's the stripiest."

"You bet," Blondel agreed. "Lots of pretty

pictures, hey?" He went across and scanned the view from the windows: the usual expanse of spot-lit grass stretching across to a fieldstone wall, dotted with well-tended trees and shrubs. There were Monitors standing here and there, apparently admiring the view of the night sky.

"It's Chillsville, pop. Like a joint direct from the hand of the Big Pusher in the Sky!" Pleech enthused.

"Listen," Blondel said, "we've got to get out of here." He went past him and looked along the side of the house toward the rear. Maybe it was a little darker back there and maybe not.

"You're not bagging it, gramps! I'm all for these kids! They're swingers, square threads and all! Like their word is: a pad for every cat, and a chick in every pad!"

"I thought the chicken went in the pot," Blondel corrected, "and two cars in every garage."

Pleech looked dubious. "I heard of cutting it with a little chicory and shredded Sunday funnies, but feathers are a new kick." He frowned. "What was that line about getting out of here?"

"I was pulling your leg. Go on with your reading. I was just looking for the root cellar."

"Cool it, dad." Pleech dropped the book and slouched over to stand between Blondel and the door. "You think these cubies are lining us? Like maybe it's just a ride on the dreamy?"

"I'll let you know after I cast my horoscope. Meanwhile don't go into any business deals without first checking them closely, and beware of smooth-talking Capricorns." Blondel started past Pleech, who put his back against the wall by the door. One hand dipped inside his black shirt and came out with a three-inch spring blade. He pointed it at Blondel and curved his mouth in a cat-smile.

"Don't go making no waves, pops," he said. His tone was a lot more businesslike now. "What's with the snoop routine? You not splitting without saying hang loose?"

"How'd they happen to pick you up?" Blondel stalled.

"Some flattie in yellow threads like bugs me, man. I bugged him back. But that was when I didn't dig the scene. Now I can see its Groovesville all the way. Like, we're in, dad. So don't go breaking the scene with no like reactionary hang-ups."

"I hear they plan to remove our brains and install monkey glands. That might boost your I.Q. a little, but would it be the real you?"

"Hand me back my leg, man. Me and old Jitters are making it good; we're like pals. And lay off the cracks about my intellect, which it's of the highest." He poked the knife out just far enough; Blondel brought a hard chop down on the pressure point just below the elbow. Pleech yipped and the knife dropped; when he ducked for it, Blondel gave him a sharp knee under the ear. Pleech went backward and sat up holding his jaw.

"You knocked my tooth out," he reported.

"Put it under your pillow for the good fairy to find," Blondel suggested. "Now you'd better move over to that closet." He indicated a door across the room. Pleech rolled his eyes and hunched his way back to it. Inside, there were shelves stacked with paper and office supplies, including two-inch paper tape. Blondel bound Pleech's wrists and ankles with the latter, then strapped his hands behind him.

"Open up," he ordered. Pleech gave him a startled look and dropped his jaw. "Hey—"

"Thanks." Blondel jammed an art-gum inside, then taped his mouth, not neglecting a couple of loops over the mop of hair and under the chin.

"You may have to shave the beard to get rid of that," he advised, "but try to think of it as being better than a cut throat." Blondel shoved the trussed collaborator in among the duplicator fluid cans on the floor and went softly back out into the silent hall.

Blondel followed the corridor back past the dining room, took a right turn, and found himself in the kitchen. A fat man with apple cheeks and a white chef's cap beamed at him and went on kneading a table full of dough. Blondel backed out, soft-footed on along the hall, through a dark room full of potted rubber plants and marble-topped tables, emerged in a room with fancy chandeliers, and a set of curtained French doors that opened silently onto a terrace. A pair of red coleus plants in wooden tubs provided a patch of dense shadow in which to stand.

Out on the lawn, Monitors strolled in leisurely fashion, taking the evening air. Beyond them, the huge, dark barrier of the hedge loomed, fifty yards away.

Blondel waited for a moment when the coast was relatively clear, then hitched up his pants, swallowed hard, stepped out and headed across the lawn at a brisk walk. He had covered about half the distance before somebody called—yelled would be too strong a word. Blondel put his head down and sprinted. He zigged and zagged to confuse any tacklers, made the bushes with the kind of spurt that wins gold medals under more favorable circumstances, and was slamming through tough thorny stuff that ripped at him like fine-gauge barbed wire. He ploughed on, bounced off a denser mass of rubbery branches and leaves, clawed his way through a barrier like the fence around the nurses' quarters at a hardship post. Twice he went down hard, but came up still digging, finally burst through into the clear and was back on the lawn, six feet from where he had first dived into the hedge, watching no more than fifty stalwart young athletes in gold suits converging from three sides. He backed a step, took a gouge in the hip pocket from the thorns, tried a dash to the right. A Monitor loomed before him, friendly smile in place, one hand upraised. Blondel ducked under it, pelted for the front of the house.

At that moment, with an ominous rumble, something large and dim in the gloom burst through the hedge directly in his path. He shied, saw light glint on an armored prow above rubber-shod tracks. There was a dull *woof!* and a white mist jetted from orifices low on the tank's sides. Blondel caught a whiff of fresh-cut hollyhocks, turned to run in a new direction, felt himself keeling over slowly like a wax figure left too long in the sun. On all fours he saw the heavy machine lumber forward, halt beside him. A hatch popped up and a dark figure jumped down, bent over him. He tried to gather his strength for a swing, fell on his face instead. Hands gripped his arms, pulled him to his feet. His eyes focussed on a pair of boots, sole-up on the lawn, connected to a set of yellow-clad legs. There was another supine Monitor beyond the first, two more in sight beyond him. . . .

Then the hands dragged him back, lifted him, thrust him through a narrow opening into dim light, dumped him on cold metal and webbing. There was a deep-throated roar, a surge of motion as the canopy thumped down, cutting off the flow of cold air.

"About time," someone was saying over the rumble of engines. "We've been hovering in the underbrush for six hours, waiting for you to show yourself."

Blondel got a firm grip on his head, swung it around far enough to see a curly head of dark hair and a set of horn-rims.

"Hey," he said weakly. "This is . . . I was . . . you were . . ."

"Take it easy," Maxwell said. "You didn't think we'd run out on you, did you?"

CHAPTER FIVE

After a quarter of an hour, the fumes had cleared sufficiently from Blondel's head to enable him to sit up and look around at a corrugated metal floor, a padded curve of door, the clear plastic canopy and a spread of lighted instrument faces before which Maxwell and another man sat, hunched forward over a small screen that threw a theatrical light on their faces. Blondel saw that it was an illuminated map, unreeling steadily across the frame. Maxwell glanced up. "Ah, you're feeling better," he called over the shrill of wind and the roar of the engines.

"I guess so. What's going on?"

Maxwell pointed to a glowing blue dot at the center of the screen.

"This is our present location. We made the pickup here"—he indicated a spot on the map—"and our destination is to the north of here." He tapped the upper edge of the screen.

Blondel fought back a sensation of seasickness induced by the swaying, bobbing motion of the vehicle. "This is quite a machine you've got here," he said. "Who owns it, the Army?"

Maxwell patted it affectionately. "Our Z-car has been quite a little surprise to the enemy. Radar-negative, nuclear-powered, impregnably armored. Nothing they've got can touch it." He frowned. "Everything works but the guns. I'll have to speak to the General about that."

"General who?"

Maxwell pursed his lips, cast an oblique look at Blondel. "After what you've been through, I assume you're ready to join the fight in an active capacity?"

"Um," Blondel said. Maxwell nodded, as though this were the countersign. "As I told you earlier," he said, "there were some of us who were not entirely unprepared for the present situation."

"By the way, what *is* the present situation?" Blondel cut in. "How much of a beachhead have they established? What's our side doing?"

"The enemy controls New York, Philly, Boston—the whole eastern seaboard, as far as we've been able to reconnoiter," Maxwell said gruffly. "Every city and town seems to have its quota of the scoundrels."

"Where have we hit back? Are their troops on the move? Any armor? What about air action? Any infantry dropping in to secure the ground?"

"Curiously, they seem content for the present merely to, er, occupy the country," Maxwell conceded.

"*They*'re content? What about us—has there been much bloodshed?"

Maxwell shook his head. "Not yet—insofar as we know."

"What's the Pentagon doing?"

"Nothing." Maxwell clamped his jaw. "There hasn't been a peep from Washington. We *did* have a verbal report from a pair of refugee bureaucrats that the capital is heavily invested by the enemy and that the President was last seen headed west in a used station wagon—but of course, that's merely hearsay."

"What about our allies—Britain, Liberia, Tierra del Fuego?"

"You forgot Lebanon." Maxwell looked grave. "All occupied, it appears. None of them have cashed their first-of-the-month aid checks."

"This is *really* serious!" Blondel exclaimed.

Just then the radio went *beep!* and a fruity voice said: *"Hi, fans! This is Happy Horinip, with your latest Progress Bulletin! It's a pleasure to report that Block 354, Zone 67—remember to look at your wall chart, if the new terminology is still a little confusing—Block 354 is the winner of this hour's co-op award!*

Yes sir, Block 354 has topped some keen competition to fulfill their registration quota a record four minutes, twelve seconds early! Congrats, Block 354, and there'll be an official Quota Toppers club emblem and pennant on the way to you. . . ."

"Is that . . .?"

"That's them," Maxwell said grimly over the patter. "They've adopted this approach on all their late-night spots. Early in the morning, they use what we've designated the HTM—Hi There Moms—format, and at 4:46 P.M. they switch to code AYC—All Your Commuters. Our top psych men are trying to crack the implication of it but, so far, no luck."

". . . now for a couple of requests." The Monitor's voice was still registering barely suppressed elation. *"Here's a card signed Bunny and Whitey . . ."* Maxwell whipped out a notebook, began writing, his head cocked to the speaker.

"Bunny," he muttered. "We're compiling a master list of collaborationists," he said over his shoulder. "Whitey. . . . We already have over seven hundred thousand names on it, and that's after less than thirty-six hours." He closed the book with a snap and looked resolute. "After the Liberation, we'll see about some of these fellow travelers."

"What outfit are you with?" Blondel yelled over the thump and jangle of the record Bunny and Whitey had requested.

"Blondel, have you ever heard of the Spe-

cial Counter Retaliatory Action Group?"
Maxwell looked solemn.

"Nope."

"We in SCRAG," Maxwell said, "have, for over two years, had as our prime mission preparation for the inevitable day of contact with a technologically superior power. This vehicle in which we're now traveling"— he thumped it—"is merely one example of the sort of thing we've held in reserve for the crisis."

"SCRAG—is that some kind of governmental department?"

Maxwell pushed his lips out, indicating cautious confirmation. "Actually, our funds have come in part from, ah, private contributions, with the balance made up through a special allocation to the Summer Program of Leisure-Time Undertakings for Retired Government Employees."

"I think I've heard of that one." Blondel nodded. " 'A Sunnier Senility for Senior Civil Servants.' Isn't that their motto?"

"Something like that. At any rate, suffice it to say that virtually unlimited funds and the best efforts of some of the finest brains in the country have gone to prepare the Group to meet any threat the Enemy could throw at us. As you can see, this vehicle is a special model, superior to anything our armed forces have at their disposal; all of our equipment is equally advanced."

"Why don't the Army and the Air Force have it?"

Maxwell looked astounded. "My God, man, you know as well as I the military services are riddled with subversives!"

"Oh."

"No." Maxwell nodded. "SCRAG knows how to keep her secrets. Our network of underground installations were planned and constructed with a view to maximum security combined with optimum strike capability. Of course we've suffered from a chronic shortage of qualified personnel, but we've always felt that a small elite cadre was preferable to an unwieldy roster of unreliables."

Blondel cleared his throat and tried to look reliable.

Maxwell cocked an eye at him. "I've seen you in action, Blondel," he said crisply. "I like your style. I know a one-hundred-percent American when I see one."

"Of course my parents *were* immigrants," Blondel confided. "But maybe you'll forgive that."

"Say, don't get the wrong idea about us." Maxwell chuckled tolerantly. "SCRAG isn't some kind of wild-haired extremist group out to make the world safe for blue-eyed Protestants. We don't give a damn about a man's race, color, or creed. All we're interested in is his loyalty to his country." His chin got firm. "And I think we can agree that anyone who wants to hand this nation over to a foreign power to run needs his marbles counted."

"Any idea where these lads in yellow come from?" Blondel countered. "What kind of fire-power they're holding in reserve, if the spot commercials don't do the job for them?"

Maxwell nodded. "We've definitely pinpointed their origin as being somewhere east of the Urals. We've got some pretty fancy radar-type gear that recorded their blips almost three minutes before the moment at which their landings took place: 3:26 P.M., Eastern Daylight Saving Time, last Wednesday."

"Oh." Blondel scratched his chin. "How did you know where I was?"

"I planted a sounder on you." Maxwell smiled wisely. "Subcutaneous, little needle the size of a human hair."

The raucous sounds from the radio stopped, and five seconds of silence ensued. Then: "Mr. Blondel," the Tersh Jetterax's voice came from the speaker, "I'm most disappointed that you left us before viewing the remainder of the orientation. I feel that we were making splendid progress. It is, after all, men of action like yourself whom we need most urgently in our task of bringing the New Dawn to your people. Since you wish so strongly to leave us, I shan't press the point. But if you should change your mind, simply notify one of your friendly Monitors."

"Oh-oh, I'll bet they're on our tail," Blondel hissed in Maxwell's ear.

"No—radar's clear. They know better than

to tangle with one of our Z-cars." Maxwell was eyeing Blondel with sudden suspicion. "That chap seems to think you planned to defect."

"Well—he did try to recruit me," Blondel said, "but I didn't sign anything."

"Ummm . . . That's not good, Blondel. Did they use any drugs on you, any electronic devices—flashing lights, monotonous voices, that sort of thing?"

"They showed me a few pictures and tried to sell me on a retraining program," Blondel conceded. "But it was pretty routine stuff."

"Describe it."

Blondel delivered a five-minute briefing on Frokinil's plans for developing the population's latent talents.

"Tap dancing, eh?" Maxwell frowned and chewed his lip. "The General isn't going to like this."

"I wasn't crazy about it myself."

"Well . . . we'll have to defer any decision until the General's seen you."

"Decision about what?"

"About your future usefulness to SCRAG, of course."

"Oh." Fighting a slight uneasiness, Blondel made himself comfortable with his back to the wall and watched the map unreel as the car headed northwest over rough ground at a speed he estimated at something over 100 MPH.

*   *   *

He awoke stiff and fuzz-eyed from a dream of being sent over Niagara Falls in a barrel of cement, groped his way out into crusty snow and a temperature that would have seemed mild to a Polar bear. Across a wide sweep of tracked white a big rustic lodge, built of logs like a Viking mead hall, reared up against a backdrop of blue-black spruce and star-sequined sky. There were lights in the building, and more lights bobbing around outside it. A carbon arc on a derrick built of timber cut a path across to where he stood. Maxwell made semaphoring motions with his arms and it swung away. A dog was barking somewhere, and a man's voice was calling someone's name. The sounds had the edge-irritating quality that such things take on with insufficient sleep.

Maxwell told Blondel to follow him; together they stamped across the snow, went up on a wide porch with benches and ski racks, and a big iron-banded door with a round pink-and-yellow glass in it. A small, plump man in shirt-sleeves was holding it open and hugging himself.

Inside, there were steps up to a broad hall with coat racks loaded with mackinaws and parkas; then more steps led down into a big roughhewn room with a high beam ceiling, all dark wood and antlers and Indian rugs. The fireplace at the far end was ten feet wide, faced with fieldstone; in it a pair of six-foot logs blazed away like the Chicago fire. A tall, lean, high-shouldered man stood with his back to the flames, feet planted apart, hands behind his back. He wore riding breeches and boots, and a red flannel shirt open to show gray winter underwear at the neck. His face was vague against the light; but he seemed to have a thick, Mussolini-type nose, a straight line for a mouth, thick slicked-back white hair and a jaw like a power shovel—not big, but capable of biting hard.

Maxwell went across to him, swung around to wave a hand at Blondel in a gesture like an MC introducing a featured act.

"General Blackwish, Mr. Blondel."

The general gave Blondel an up-and-down look, then did a right-face and took three steps, executed a left about-face and came back, finished off with a snappy right-face and came back to parade rest.

"You want to be a member of the SCRAG team, do you, Blondel?" His voice was startlingly high and thin, almost a falsetto.

"Well, not exactly, General," Blondel said. "Actually, I was sort of thinking I'd just grab a night's sleep and be on my way." Blondel gave Blackwish a hopeful smile; the general's look shriveled it in mid-air. "To Ecuador, maybe," Blondel amplified. His voice seemed to have a loud, lonely sound in his own ears. "On personal business . . ."

Blackwish had thick black brows that grew in a heavy bar. His eyes looked out from the shadows like a matched pair of black opal stickpins. They bored into Blondel's face for a full ten-second count, then flicked past him to Maxwell.

"General, I think Blondel's a little tired—" Maxwell started.

"Colonel, I understood you to describe the pickup as a highly-motivated, loyal American!" The general's voice had gone a tone or two higher and acquired an edge like a meat saw.

"Well, now, General, I'm sure that what Blondel meant was—"

"Personal business, eh?" Blackwish drowned him out. "His country invaded by a foreign power dedicated to the destruction of the American Way of Life, and he's concerned about his overseas business interests! You call that Americanism?"

"Well, it's not exactly business interests, General," Blondel soothed. "More of a job. Actua—"

"What job can compare with the duty of hurling the borsht-and-vodka-swilling enemy back from our shores?" Blackwish's face had moved forward until his nose was six inches from Blondel's. He caught an aroma of Scotch mingled with a ruggedly masculine after shave. "You're content to hear the tramp of booted foreign feet in your country's peaceful streets? The jabber of alien voices in the shrines of Democracy? The thunder of gunfire, mowing down your fellow Americans?"

"They speak English," Blondel pointed out. "And I haven't seen them shoot anybody—"

"That's beside the point!" Blackwish raised both hands as if to call down lightnings. "They're invaders! Do you realize that this is the first time since the birth of our nation that the tramp of booted foreign feet has sounded in our peaceful streets?"

"Well, the British got as far as Washington—"

"And were hurled into the sea! Would you tuck your tail between your legs now, with the jabber of alien voices sounding in the shrines of Democracy, and scuttle off to safety in wherever-it-was?"

"I thought maybe I'd give it a try, inasmuch as the Air Force—"

"Riddled with subversives!" Blackwish shrilled. "Went over to the enemy in a body! Not a sortie's been flown, not a bomb dropped, while the enemy swills borsht and vodka on U.S. soil and their guns mow down loyal Americans, unresisted!"

"Ah, General," Maxwell eased a word in edgeways. "I think what Mr. Blondel meant was—"

"You sponsored this fellow, brought him here, to my secret headquarters!" Blackwish blasted him down. "What's your excuse, Colonel? You know security regulations!"

"Yes, indeed, General. I just wanted to point out that Mr. Blondel *did* wreck an enemy chopper, and that he . . ." Maxwell shot Blondel a look pregnant with obscure meanings, ". . . penetrated enemy headquarters at Pulaski and brought out important intelligence regarding their brainwashing scheme."

Blackwish opened his mouth and closed it with a snap like a carp taking a bare hook.

"Brainwashing scheme?"

"It's insidious as hell, sir," Maxwell said admiringly. "The idea seems to be that they'll offer to teach grease monkeys to become ballet dancers and, er, acrobats, and thus lure them into their toils—"

"What self-respecting grease monkey would want to become a toe dancer?" the general bellowed. "Don't these fellows know they're dealing with Americans?"

"That's just a rough idea, of course," Maxwell said quickly. "Blondel can fill you in on the whole picture."

"Well, what about it?" Blackwish snapped his eyes at Blondel. "Never mind the window dressing. What have they got in the way of firepower?"

"I didn't see any guns, but maybe they don't need them. They've got other things."

"Such as?"

Blondel described the eerie experience of being walked from his car as though his legs belonged to someone else. "And to judge from the tricks they can play with radios and TV's, it's a safe bet they've got more up their sleeves than we've seen so far."

"Is that *all* you learned, Mr. Blondel?"

Blackwish showed him a set of square-cut store teeth.

"Just about—plus the fact that they seem eager not to do any damage."

"Hmmph! Indeed!" Blackwish snapped his fingers. A bow-legged nautical type, who had been hovering in the wings, came over.

"Bring me File Y," the general commanded.

The trio stood in chilly silence, listening to the fire crackle, while Blackwish took two more turns up and down the quarter-deck. The sailor came back and handed him a black leather folder as big as a Chinese menu. He snapped it open.

"Less than seventy-two hours after initial contact, the enemy had demolished over forty-one square miles of Metropolitan New York," he said crisply, and flipped the page. "In Philadelphia, twenty-one square miles of the municipal area have been similarly razed." He flipped another page. "In Boston, fifteen square miles. The figures are approximate, of course."

"They've blasted the cities?" Blondel frowned.

"There, ah, wasn't necessarily any actual bloodshed," Maxwell put in, then faded back under Blackwish's glare.

"No actual bombs were employed, it appears," the general said grudgingly. "Some sort of, er, instantaneous, ah, disintegrator ray was employed—if any reports are correct." He closed the folder.

"Could I see that, General?" Blondel held out a hand. Blackwish put the folder behind him. "Certainly not! This is classified material!"

"In that case, I guess I don't believe you," Blondel said. "Disintegrator rays, yet." He folded his arms and looked scornful.

Blackwish bridled like a southern matron encountering a colored citizen in the front of the bus.

"You're questioning my word?"

"I don't know you from Adam," Blondel pointed out. "Maxwell here has dropped a few dark hints that your outfit is responsible for the last few unbalanced national budgets; but that's just talk. What are you a general in, the Salvation Army?"

"I hold my commission as Brigadier-General of State Militia," Blackwish snarled. "I'm hardly accountable to a civilian—"

"Er, Mr. Blondel has been through a lot, General," Maxwell interjected. "His nerves are frayed. I think we ought to forget this little meeting—we seem to have gotten off on a couple of bad feet—and get together in the morning, eh?"

"I'd like to see the proof that the Monitors have actually wiped out our cities," Blondel said. "Then maybe there'll be something to talk about."

Blackwish sucked in a breath—about a bellow and a half's worth—but Maxwell slid smoothly into the gap: "That's easy enough, eh, General? We're in dire need of good men, here at SCRAG—and, naturally, a man has a right to know the enemy. Why don't we just show him the photos, sir, let him grasp the full extent of the atrocities these fellows have carried out while prating of peace and good will?"

Blackwish grunted, worked his lips around a little, then shoved the folder at Maxwell. Maxwell opened it and pulled out an eight-by-ten, black-and-white glossy, passed it over to Blondel. It was a clear shot from about ten thousand feet, obscured by a little early evening haze and a king-sized fingerprint. But it showed clearly that the city of New York looked like a dingy birthday cake with a rectangular slice lifted out of the middle. The edges of the annihilated area were as smooth and straight as if they had been planed off by a power mower, leaving a vacant stretch as clean as a morgue slab.

"Philadelphia," Maxwell said crisply, and handed over a second shot. This time the wiped-out area was in a thick L shape, taking in a good half of the city. The view of Boston was equally discouraging.

"These were shot about eight hours ago," Maxwell said. "Just before we set out to collect you."

"How did you manage to get that close? They've got blimps and copters."

"For some reason we haven't yet cracked, they don't molest our copters except to render the firearms aboard inoperative."

"Were there any military objectives in those areas?"

"None whatever," Maxwell said flatly.

"Those were some of the most densely-populated urban areas on the North American continent!" Blackwish stated heatedly. "Uncounted thousands of our fellow citizens have been rendered homeless by this dastardly act of unprovoked ferocity!"

"I wonder what the point was?"

"I think that's clear enough!" Blackwish snorted. "This was intended as a warning—a sample of the brutal power and vicious intent of the invader! But they underestimate the fighting spirit of America! Rather than intimidating us, these barbaric acts serve only to reinforce our determination to throw the borsht-and-vodka-swilling scoundrels into the sea!"

"That's only a part of the picture," Maxwell contributed. "According to their own admissions, they've closed down every school in the country. The hospitals have been taken over and placed under what we've termed a gauze curtain, with all admissions controlled by the enemy. The same with the prisons; they boast of having released vast numbers of psychotic killers on the streets—"

"Claim to have cured 'em," Blackwish piped up. "Tommyrot! You don't cure that kind of human debris! If I had my way, we'd put an end to coddling and make more use of the death penalty!"

"Our computers indicate that no more

than two hundred thousand troops have been landed so far," Maxwell stated. "The time for our counterstrike is now, before they're massively reinforced."

Blackwish rubbed his hands together. "These fellows are in for a little surprise! They imagine we're beaten, cowering to the tramp of booted foreign feet and the thunder of enemy gunfire—"

"And the jabber of alien voices in the shrines," Maxwell reminded him.

"Well put, Maxwell. But we have a trick or two up our sleeves, eh, Colonel?"

"Right, sir!"

"What kind of surprise were you thinking of, General?" Blondel queried.

"During the past two years, we've not been idle," Blackwish stated, nodding in agreement with what he was saying. "Our laboratories—the finest in the land, manned by scrupulously reliable personnel, all with impeccable security records, of course— have come up with a number of devices which will make the invader regret the day that he left his borsht and vodka to tackle America!"

"You must have an impressive complex of-laboratories," Blondel commented. "Where are they?"

"In the basement, of course."

"You mean—just one basement?"

"Well, our boys didn't exactly *invent* anything," Maxwell clarified. "We tended to concentrate our emphasis on technical intelligence work, and I think I can say that our chaps are among the most adept in the field."

"They've rifled the files of every supersecret agency in the government." Blackwish almost beamed. "Turned up some remarkable items, buried in the vaults by the subversives who have been entrusted with the nation's security." He rubbed his hands together.

"Well, what about it Blondel? Are you with us? Do you want a part in the Great Struggle? Are you an American patriot, or are you not?"

"I have a feeling a new design for a WAC's brassiere isn't going to help much," Blondel said. "Or, for that matter, a vest pocket H-bomb. Technically, these Monitors are out in front like a co-ed's frat pin."

"Hah! You jape, sir!" Blackwish looked triumphant. "But we hold a weapon in reserve which will exceed your wildest expectations—and those of the enemy as well!"

"And we're pretty sure it will be undetectable," Maxwell added. "It employs an entirely new destructive principle—and it's small enough to carry in your coat pocket."

"I don't see what good tossing hand grenades is going to do," Blondel objected. "The Monitors are scattered all over the country, and I don't think they're going to stand around and let you sneak up on them one at a time."

"Grenades, pah!" Blackwish chirped. "This

is no toy, sir, but a weapon of truly hellish power!"

"And we don't plan to pop off Monitors one at a time," Maxwell put in. "We're carrying out an intensive search for their headquarters; not the little field HQ from which I plucked you, Blondel, but their central base of operations. When we do—blooie!"

"I think you've said enough," Blackwish announced. "More than enough. It's time Mr. Blondel declared himself. What about it, sir? Are you with us—or against us?"

"General, I think you're going at the whole thing wrong," Blondel told him. "Even if you could blow Monitors up wholesale—which I doubt, frankly—it's not a move that's likely to do our side any good. Up to now they've kept things on a high plane—lots of propaganda, but no firing squads. But if you succeed in murdering some of them—"

"Bah, sir! We've no time for the counsels of mollycoddles! They've asked for violence! They'll get it by God, with bells on!"

"All you'll do is stir up reprisals. What we need is a grass-roots resistance movement. If you'll use your Z-cars to distribute leaflets urging passive resistance—"

"That's enough!" Blackwish yelled. "Don't imagine you can spread your defeatist doctrines here!" He had a bark like a Pekinese pushed off its favorite pillow. "We know how to deal with fifth columnists—"

"Ah, General, sir," Maxwell stepped in.

"Don't be hasty, now; after all, Blondel hasn't yet said—"

"Then speak up, sir!"

"Suppose you do hit them—or try to—and fail to knock them out?" Blondel asked.

"Then, at least, we'll have shown them that we're not a nation of weaklings—quitters who'll give up their land without a struggle!"

"A suicide mission won't help matters. Now, if—"

"It would teach them a decent respect for American patriots!"

"The more they respect us, the harder they'll fight. Why don't we let them go on thinking we're softies, and then—"

"For God's sake, Blondel, tell him you'll join up!" Maxwell hissed.

"You fellows don't seem to get the picture," Blondel protested. "The Monitors could squash us like bugs if they wanted to. For some reason they don't seem to want to. I'm against doing anything that might change their minds."

Blackwish reached for his hip pocket, produced an automatic. "There are direct methods for dealing with treason," he snarled. "I don't know what your masters imagined they could accomplish by sending you here, but—"

"Now hold on a second, General." Blondel managed to get the words past a sudden constriction in his throat. Blackwish was holding the gun as steady as a corpse's smile.

"General," Maxwell got in, "may I respectfully suggest you not shoot him until we've all had time to get a little better acquainted? We don't actually *know* he's a spy—and he *is* an experienced pilot—just the man we need for you-know-what."

"Pah!" Blackwish lowered the pistol, pushed the safety on, thrust it back in his pocket. "At best, the man's an arrant coward and a defeatist, Maxwell! I can't understand how he was able to hoodwink you into bringing him here. However, for the present I'll permit you to take him downstairs and lock him up until I decide what disposition to make of him."

"Lock him up, sir? But, sir—"

"I have a number of captured German technicians on my staff who'll have the answers out of him in jigtime! Afterward—"

"But, General, I brought Blondel here to recruit him, not scare him to death!"

"Colonel, this headquarters is in a state of full War Emergency, condition Red Alert! I'll have no unreliables free to snoop here! Lock him up. That's an order!"

"But he's likely to get a bad impression—"

"Colonel, I still have my gun, in case you're contemplating mutiny in the face of the enemy!"

"Yes, sir." Maxwell gave Blondel a disgusted look. "Come along, Blondel. I'm afraid you've failed to make a favorable impression."

*   *   *

Blondel followed Maxwell up to a small room on the third floor under the eaves. It had knotty-pine walls, heavy rafters slanting down to a small window; a bunk bed with a patchwork quilt, and a miniature fireplace with a rag rug in front of it.

"Very homey," he said. "But I thought the General specified the basement."

"There's nothing down there but the coal bin and a room full of preserve jars," Maxwell said in a tight voice.

"And the laboratories."

"That's the coal bin."

"He might get upset and shoot you for insubordination."

"The general's a great man," Maxwell snapped. "He was the only man in the country with the vision to foresee this day. He can't help it if he acts like an idiot at times."

"You think you can talk him out of this raid?"

"Don't get the wrong idea, Blondel," Maxwell said sharply. "I'm all for the raid! It's a magnificent plan! Don't let appearances deceive you. SCRAG's new weapon is all the general said, and more!"

"Look, if you boys want to play war, that's fine; but why don't you just slip me out the back way, and—"

"Blondel, I brought you here in good faith, thinking you'd want to get into the fight. Perhaps I was wrong—but I'm still a loyal member of the SCRAG team. I feel a certain responsibility for you—but don't fool yourself, I'd shoot you down myself if I thought there was anything in the general's idea that you're a traitor or spy."

"Just a suggestion," Blondel said cheerfully.

"Get some rest," Maxwell ordered. "Perhaps in the morning you'll see things more clearly. And don't get any ideas about leaving. Our security's watertight; take my word for it."

He went out, and there were noises from the latch as though large padlocks were being hung on the door. Then footsteps retreated and left Blondel in silence.

Curled under the quilt, Blondel watched the firelight throw flickery shadows across the ceiling and listened to the wind whining around the windows, regretting his failure to sign up for the general's program—suicide raids and all, with the option of beating a tactical retreat at the first opportunity. After all, he reflected sleepily, there was nothing to keep him from putting on his birdsuit—funny, he'd forgotten how nice it was to fly—and just flit away through the open window. But first, he'd surprise the general by sailing into his room and buzzing his bed a couple of times. He was out in the hall now, cruising along effortlessly just under the ceiling. It was a long, gray hall, with lots of doors with shiny brass knobs. Blondel tried one after another, but they were all locked—which was a shame, because there were wonderful things stored there if he could just get inside. And all the time it was getting harder and harder to fly, and now he was flapping for all he was worth, but something warm and soft seemed to be engulfing him—smothering him—

"Shhh!" a feminine voice was hissing hotly in this ear, along with an aroma of Spearmint and *Nuit d'Amour*. "Do you want to escape from this kook farm, or don't you?"

CHAPTER SIX

For a long giddy moment Blondel's mental machinery revved like drag slicks on an oil patch, attempting to classify conflicting sensory impressions; then reason reasserted itself. The warm smooth shape resembling the nubile body of a naked female pressing against him under the covers was obviously a dream; therefore he was actually awake and flying, or . . .

"Well, say something," the breathy voice urged, while what seemed to be soft lips nibbled at his ear lobe. "But keep it quiet; old Blockwits is on patrol in his commando suit."

"Wha . . . who . . ." Blondel managed.

"I'm Nelda Monroe. I *used* to be a dedicated member of the SCRAG team. That was before I became aware of the true nature of the struggle between statusquoism and self-realization."

"Oh," Blondel said.

"I heard you standing up to him. I knew instantly that you were one of us."

"Who?"

"You, silly."

"I mean—who's us?"

"Who are we?"

"That's right."

"My God, I can tell already you're going to be right for me." A large, slightly damp leg was thrown over Blondel's stomach. "You see right to the heart of the essential paradox, without flinching from the answers."

"I'm afraid I don't know exactly what it is we're talking about, Miss Monroe," he told her. "When you came in you said something—"

"Shhh!" A warm hand groped for his, placed it firmly over a large bare breast. The mouth slid around the side of his neck and clamped itself over his as solidly as a toilet plunger. Blondel managed a deep breath through his nose, and felt her weight come onto him like a Sumi wrestler. "We'll talk later," she said into his tonsils. "First I want to get to feel I really know you. . . ."

Blondel gave up the struggle then and went ahead with the introductions.

Half an hour later Blondel was sitting on the edge of the bed checking for broken ribs, while Nelda curled around his hips like an oversized pink Cupid, mewing contentedly and fingering his knee.

"I'm wild for knees," she confided. "And eyebrows. And I love a bare man's torso with a wrist watch."

"That's no reason to break up the rest," Blondel pointed out. "I may have a use for it."

"God, when a fella's really *right* for me, I guess I lose my head a little. By the way, what's your name?"

"Blondel."

"Ummm. You're not Jewish?"

"If I am, mother never told me."

"Too bad. Minority groups arouse me a lot."

"What do you do with them, tear their legs off?"

"My God, you're not one of those hopeless bourgeois moralists, I hope!" She dropped his knee and sat up hard enough to boost him off onto the rag rug. She leaned over the edge and her bosom swung over him like a pair of impending dooms. "I mean, any meaningful relationship between male and female has got to encompass the physical actuality of their mutual attraction/repulsion syndrome—the death and rebirth cycle, as Crmblnsky put it. Not that I believe in a lot of that mystical crap. I mean, hell, a girl has to be free to act natural, or what *good* is it?"

"You're so right, Nelda," Blondel agreed. "It's just that I'm the frail type—"

"Hah! You resent my usurpation of the superior role, I guess! You have the idea that a portion of the population is doomed to forever be on the bottom, with you lolling at ease on top! I can see now that I made hasty judgement of you, Blondel!"

"Not at all," he tried to soothe her. "I can see that you considered the matter in depth—"

"I'm not sure you're the kind of fellow I want to escape with, at all."

"Shhh!" Shivering, Blondel rose and edged back under the quilt. Nelda gave ground grudgingly, but her toes were working their way up his shin. "Listen," Blondel urged, "I'm sorry about any little misunderstanding, but I'm sure I'm *exactly* the type of chap you want to escape with. What's your plan?"

She tossed her head, and a hank of blonde hair like a palomino's tail flopped back over a plump shoulder. "I've been saving it for the right man," she pouted.

"You mean the plan," Blondel deduced.

"What else? And when you came along, I was so sure. . . ."

"Look, Nelda, I assume you want to get out of the hands of these vigilantes as bad as I do. Let's work on that first, and work out our interpersonal relationships later."

"You *are* opposed to the insane invalidity of the traditional intersexual bias as a basis for our mores-complex? You *do* recognize that it's at the bottom of the present chaotic international contretemps?"

"Oh, certainly, ah, Nelda—"

"And you see the madness of any attempt to cure everything by violence?" She looked Blondel in the eyes; her own were immense and china blue, in a round face with an upturned nose and plump pouty lips between cheeks like apple turnovers.

"Right. They're going at it backwards—"

She grabbed Blondel's hands and thrust her chest at him. "God, I *knew* I was right about you, Blondel! Blowing them up is no good—for God's sake! We have to go to them empty-handed and simply explain that our Gestalts don't mesh! As soon as they understand the basic validity of our need for rejection of their aid at this point in our ethical development, they'll leave!"

"Ah . . . sure," Blondel confirmed. "My idea exactly. But first, we have to get clear of this place. Maxwell warned me that it's well guarded—"

"Fooie! Maxwell's an utter rectangle. I know how to leave here any time I want to."

Blondel threw back the covers. "Swell. Let's go."

Nelda pulled them back, hurled herself at him like an avalanche of foam-rubber bolsters. He fought gamely, but had to settle for another draw.

*   *   *

Half an hour later he was back on the edge of the bed, gathering his resources for another try.

"Look, Nelda, this little idyll is a memory I'll treasure always," he assured her, "but dawn comes early at this latitude, and we really ought to get moving—that is, if you really know a way out of this backwoods Buchenwald."

"There you go, with your smug masculine assumption of the unreliability of the female of the species!" Nelda flounced back under the quilt.

"OK." Blondel rose, began pulling on his clothes. "I'll try it alone."

"How can you? You don't know the way."

"I'll find one."

"God, you're so determined!" She threw off the covers. "I love a masculine-type man—"

"Not until we're out of this mess," Blondel said sternly. "Why don't you be a good girl and get into some clothes now?"

Nelda glanced down at her plump, undraped form, gave it a casual bump and grind. "The male paradox of puritanism versus sexual voracity—" she started.

"Look, kid, psychoanalyze me later, OK? For now, it's cold out there, and cute as you are, bare feet in the snow are impractical."

"Ha! Having slaked your lusts at the fountain of my compassion you now assume the jackboots of authoritarianism—"

"All right, so I put my dime in your coke

machine," Blondel said tiredly. "I guess we both got value received. Can we declare a truce in the battle of the genders and do a fast fade before Blackwish shows up with his German scientists and starts poking splinters under my fingernails?"

"He threatened torture?" Nelda gasped. She jumped up, snatched up a filmy pink and green creation from the chair, whipped it around her ample form. "My God, why didn't you say so? I won't be a minute!" She slid past the door, a pale blimp in the firelight.

Five minutes later, waiting in the darkness at the head of the narrow flight of steps leading down to the second floor, Blondel heard the creak of boards. Nelda materialized from the shadows, a spherical composition in a pink wolfskin parka, white snow-pants, and red alligator mukluks. She came close, breathed mint-flavored breath on his face.

"This way—and watch your head." Her mittened hand caught his, led him toward the end of the gallery. Blondel saw a darker rectangle open against the dark paneling. Nelda ducked through, drew him after her. Cold drafts wormed their way up his pant-legs. There was a dusty, resinous smell of wood shavings in the air.

"Be careful where you put your feet," Nelda cautioned. "If you step off the boards you'll drop into Blockwits's bedroom." She tittered. "You should see it: he's got a picture of Stonewall Jackson on the wall under crossed sabers."

"How's the bed?"

"Hard," Nelda said. "Not that I'd know," she added primly.

Blondel followed as she picked her way daintily through the pitch blackness. After a tortuous trip of some fifty feet, she made a small sound of approval and pulled Blondel forward.

"Boost me up," she directed. Blondel groped over the parka, a bulk like a long-haired molasses drum. He tried a grip just south of the estimated equator, bent his knees and pushed. Nelda giggled.

"Fresh," she said.

"Sorry." He crouched, set his shoulder under a conveniently placed bulge, heaved again. Nelda grunted.

"Well, you don't have to be rough!"

"How high do I have to lift you?" he whispered hoarsely.

"About a foot."

Blondel set himself, gripped her around the middle, leaned back and heaved hard; her weight went on him like a soft piano; her arms encircled his neck.

"My God, Blondel," she sighed in his ear, "you're so devastatingly strong! It makes me go all wilty inside—"

"Let go!" Blondel wheezed, staggering. Nelda struck the boardwalk with a shuddering crash. At once, a startled voice from the room below barked, "Eh? What's that?" Feet hit the floor. Other, more distance voices called questions.

"That did it," Blondel groaned. "We woke the whole place up."

"Humph," Nelda sniffed. "Since you choose to make a production of it, I'll just climb through by myself." There were scrapings and scufflings, a small feminine exclamation or two; Blondel reached, felt the alligator boots waving before him. Then they were drawn up and Nelda called softly: "I'm through. Hurry up!"

He found the opening, pulled himself up and was in a cold, drafty passage, faintly lit by dusty windows under the eaves, and obstructed by stacked cartons.

"This is Blockwits's Top-Secret storage room," Nelda said. "There's a stair along here. . . ."

It was a precarious ten-minute descent down almost vertical ladders nailed in position in a narrow shaft. Blondel climbed with set teeth, wincing at the haloos ringing back and forth through the house, waiting for the inevitable outcry announcing the discovery of his absence.

"We're down," Nelda hissed. Blondel dropped the last foot, looked around at the dim bulks of a wood-burning range, a massive ice chest, a wide table, stacked shelves.

"I think there's some lovely fudge in the fridge," Nelda said, "if those gluttons haven't eaten it all."

"Maybe we'd better skip the goodies for now," Blondel suggested.

"Silly, we need supplies for the trip. I won't be a minute." She tiptoed away, and Blondel went across and tried the plank door. It opened a crack to let in a frigid gust of air. He shivered, looking out at the moonlit snowfield.

"How far is the nearest town?" he whispered.

"Oh, about twenty-six miles. But there's nothing there. It's just a sort of trading post."

"Where did you plan to head for, once we're clear of the house?"

"How about Chicago?"

"Fine. How far is it?"

"Umm . . . about two hundred miles."

"That's quite a walk."

"Oh, we won't be walking. We're going to take old Blockwits's private tank."

"The Z-car?"

"Ummm. Do you prefer Cheddar or Gorgonzola?"

"Either one's fine. Where does he keep it stored?"

"In the woodshed. White or rye?"

"Rye, no caraway seeds. Do you know how to drive it?"

"No, silly. Don't you?"

"I don't know. I can try."

"Of course. Mustard?"

"Plain, no horse-radish."

"My God, I abhor horse-radish myself! Isn't that amazing?"

"We were meant to meet," Blondel admitted. "See if you can find some salami."

"Hebrew National all right?"

"Yeah—and some kosher dills."

"You're sure you're not Jewish?"

"Not actively. And some potato chips—if they're nice and crisp."

"Oh, goody, pig's knuckles."

"Not the horrible gristly kind," Blondel protested.

"My God, no, Blockwits is too much of a gourmet for anything like *that*. You *do* like onions?"

"Spanish are all right, but not those big white fellows."

"Bermudas? They give me gas, too."

"Speaking of which, I hope there's plenty of fuel in the car."

"And spring onions are just as bad."

"It sounded like a turbine. They're real gas-eaters. Where do they keep the spare number two diesel?"

"There's some kind of big tank back of the barn."

"There go the lights on in the yard." Blondel ducked back. "You and your onions! Now we'll never get to the car!"

"Certainly we will." Nelda's voice was unperturbed. Her shadow, cast by the floodlights outside, flitted across the wall as she tucked the last of the picnic lunch into a wicker hamper. "Well, shall we?"

"Good God, not again!"

"I mean leave," Nelda said indignantly.

"This way." She went to a low door set in the rear wall behind the stove, pulled it wide. "A covered passage to the woodshed for bringing in logs during a blizzard."

Blondel poked his head in. "Hmmm. Maybe this is going to work after all." He stepped in, followed the low earth-floored passage along to a right angle turn, stumbling over frozen clods in the dark. Wind whistled through the gaps in the rough board walls. Through a knothole he caught a glimpse of parka-clad men stumping across the snow, tugged by immense white dogs straining at stout chain leads.

"If they see us, it's good-by pig's knuckles," he muttered.

The passage dipped, and Blondel's feet slipped on smooth ice. Nelda squeaked and grabbed his arm.

"Don't drop the lunch," he cautioned. The ground rose again. Fifty feet further, the path ended in a heavy plank door secured by a thick black iron hasp supporting a massive padlock.

"Swell," Blondel commented. "Any other ideas?"

"I've got the key." Nelda pressed past him, unlocked the door, pushed it back.

Inside the woodshed, Blondel squinted through the gloom at the squatting, stream-lined bulk of the Z-car, parked close under an immense stack of split cordwood. He worked his way around to the driver's side, cautiously opened the door, slid into the bucket seat, looked over the maze of controls. A large red button labelled START caught his eye.

"Come on," he hissed. "We may as well try it before they find us—"

"Oh, dear," Nelda whispered. "Look—quick!"

Blondel jumped from the car, stumbled across to her side, peered through the indicated gap between boards. A bulky figure in a shiny black leather jacket was approaching from the house. A big nose under black eyebrows was visible between the fleece-lined wings of the turned-up collar.

"It's Blackwish," he whispered. "If he ever thinks to look in here . . ."

"Not him," Nelda said. "He's probably got his minions out climbing trees. He never does anything the easy way."

"I guess he just needs firewood then," Blondel said. "Here he comes. . . ."

"My God!" Nelda grabbed Blondel's arm and pulled. "We'll have to go back!"

"Not on your life." Blondel picked up a stout two-foot billet, took a position beside the door. Nelda made a sound like a trout deprived of air. "Blondel! You know how I condemn physical violence . . . !"

"Me too, kid," Blondel agreed. "Let's hope he doesn't commit any."

The door rattled and swung in. There was a sound of hoarse breathing. Then: "Mr. Blondel?" a shrill whisper came.

"Huh?" Blondel grunted, and Nelda yipped.

"Ah, very good." General Blackwish stepped boldly inside. "I'm glad to see my confidence in you was not misplaced, my boy."

"Yes, it's one of the great tragedies of our time that a soldier like myself faces not only the threat of a shrewd and merciless enemy, but treachery within his own organization as well." Blackwish nodded sadly.

"What makes you think you can trust *me*?" Blondel demanded.

"Maxwell was a good man once," Blackwish said nostalgically. "But the rot has touched him: ambition." He sighed. "Fancies he's the man to replace me."

"Oh, I wouldn't say that, General. Maxwell always speaks very highly of you."

"He does?" Blackwish's eyes caught the light. "Tell me just what he said, word for word."

"Well, he said that just because you talked like an idiot—"

"Hah!"

"No, you're getting the wrong idea. He says you're a great man. He told me so when he locked me in the attic."

"Attic? Don't you mean the basement?"

"No, he said it was too damp down there. He fixed me up with a nice little room on the top floor."

"Insubordination!" Blackwish boomed. "But—how did you get my note?"

"What note?"

"If you didn't get it, how did you know to await me here?"

"We didn't. Frankly, we were escaping."

"Security leaks!" Blackwish paused to gnaw the end of his mustache. "A purge is obviously called for—but never mind that. The point is, you're here." He clapped a hand on Blondel's shoulder. "The future of the cause of 140 proof Americanism is riding on your shoulders tonight, sir! There's no one else I can trust! I'm a virtual prisoner in my own headquarters! But when you've carried the word to my loyal lieutenants, the backsliders in my organization will wish they'd scuttled to the protection of their borsht-and-vodka-swilling comrades before they set out to subvert the cause of patriotism!"

"Why don't you carry the word yourself? Frankly, I had other plans—"

"Unfortunately, I don't, er, drive," the general admitted.

"You don't . . . drive?"

"I never learned." Blackwish straightened to a position of attention as he made the confession. "Oh, I ride, mind you," he added.

"So you can't operate the Z-car?"

"I leave all that to subordinates."

"I was hoping you could show me how," Blondel said disappointedly. "Oh, well, I suppose I can figure it out."

"I wouldn't try it," the general advised. "It's booby-trapped. There's a dummy starting button wired to six kilos of TNT. Better take the copter."

Blondel's mouth opened and closed silently three or four times.

"But ..." Blackwish looked mysterious, "I have an alternate proposal."

"What's that?"

"Carry my message to my loyal lieutenants—and I'll tell you how to get clear."

"Well ..."

"Tell him to drop dead," Nelda suggested.

"Without my help you'll never make it," Blackwish pointed out.

"All right. I guess I haven't got much choice."

"Your word of honor?"

"Given. Now—"

"Cross your heart?"

"Yeah, yeah—"

"You *are* a pilot?" Blackwish queried.

Blondel nodded. "I can fly anything that's not bolted to a concrete foundation," he stated. "What have you got?"

"A Lotzafun *Poopsie*, two-passenger job, amored, radar-negative, turbo-boosters, heat and music, a clean one-owner job."

"I don't want to buy it; just borrow it."

"Sorry. I used to be in the used car game, back in quieter times. Guess I just got carried away. It's in the barn."

"Can we get to it without being seen?"

"I'll take care of everything."

"I thought you said they'd taken you prisoner."

"Nothing so direct. It's a subtler type of treason. They still pretend to follow orders, but I've seen the sly exchange of glances, heard the whispers behind hands."

"Why didn't you just turn me loose openly, then?"

"Hah! And play into their hands?"

"Where will I find these lieutenants of yours?"

"Classified," Blackwish snapped. He reached to an inner pocket, drew out a folded paper secured by a thick deposit of sealing wax. "Sealed orders. Don't open them until you're in Chicago. In case of imminent capture, eat them."

Blondel crinkled the heavy documents in his fingers. "That might take a while."

"Eat page four first," the general directed. "Skip page six. It's a list of a few bottled goods I'd like to have smuggled in, but don't bother with that—unless you've got gobs of time. The war effort comes first."

"Let's go," Nelda suggested. "My feet are cold."

"I'll go back to the house and give the all clear," Blackwish said. "Wait until you see the front porch light blink off and on six times in a row, then head for the barn. It will be unlocked."

"Don't take all night," Nelda pouted. "We'd have been gone by now, if you hadn't been helping us."

"Quite possibly, my dear." Blackwish smiled grimly. "Though not perhaps as quietly as you might have wished, eh, Blondel?"

"My feet are a little cold, too," he muttered.

"Firm up your nerve, man." Blackwish opened the door. "I, and you, and a few other dedicated individuals are all that stand between our traditional freedoms and the tramp of foreign feet in the shrines of Democracy and the jabber of alien voices in our peaceful American streets!"

"And the thunder of enemy guns, mowing down Democrats and Republicans," Blondel added.

"You have a surprising flair for eloquence," Blackwish approved. "Carry on." He stepped out and closed the door. At once a voice sounded nearby.

"General! We've been looking for you!"

"What was he doing in the woodshed?" another voice inquired.

"Merely checking on the Z-car," Blackwish replied in a bland tone. "You've seen nothing of the quarry, I assume?"

"Sure; we've got 'em cornered in the top of a sugar pine six hundred yards north-northeast."

"The hell you say," voice number two challenged. "They're holed up in a draw three hundred and fifteen yards east by south. I'm sending a team over with smudges to smoke 'em out right now."

"Fine work, men." Blackwish's voice faded as the men moved off.

"My God," Nelda said softly. "He *is* a masculine personality isn't he? There's something about him that arouses the elemental female in me."

"Have you ever tried compiling a list of things that have that effect?" Blondel inquired.

"Jealous?" Nelda's bulk bellied up to Blondel. Her mittened hand slid over his chest. "You men are such essentially reactionary creatures. You view females as no more than property, available at your whim, but otherwise relegated to a distinctly secondary role in affairs. . . ." Her lips nibbled at his chin. "My God, you lusty brute, why don't you say what you're thinking . . . ?"

"I wish I had a big Cuban sandwich with plenty of onions," Blondel parried, edging sideways. "I missed my dinner."

"You're sublimating," Nelda accused. "But there's no need for this ritualistic Judeo-Christian self-denial. We've got time for a quickie—"

"Swell. I'll have mine on whole-wheat—"

"—before Blockwits gives the signal—"

"—and easy on the bologna—"

"—and we have to go out in the cold snow—"

"—because I can't stand those little round peppers, can you?"

"—and risk our lives."

"Nonsense. It's perfectly safe!"

"That's my lover-boy!" Nelda lunged, and boards creaked against Blondel's back.

"I mean out in the snow. . . ."

"Naughty boy! I'd catch my death."

"I didn't mean—"

"This damned zipper's stuck."

"There goes the signal!"

Blondel reached the door three feet in advance, bounded through it and out across the yard with the pink Teddy-bear form of Nelda at his heels.

CHAPTER SEVEN

The SCRAG copter was a compact turbo-powered affair, hidden, as Blackwish had said, under a screen of pine boughs. It creaked dolefully as it took Nelda's weight. Blondel squeezed himself in beside her overflowing bulk, checked over the controls, started up. The machine lifted promptly, not without certain evidence of distress from the groaning rotors, and Blondel set course due south.

Two hours passed in nervous silence. Then Blondel, squinting ahead, said "Ah," and pointed. In the predawn gloom, the mighty glow of Chicago provided a beacon visible from fifty miles distant. No Monitors interfered with their cautious approach across the lake. Peering out through a light mist, Nelda made a surprised noise.

"Things look different! I don't see any lights along the waterfront; or at least not the usual ones. It looks more like a lot of little Christmas trees. . . ."

"Probably blacked-out," Blondel grunted.

"And there are big blank patches beyond," she cried.

"Sure—Blackwish told me about the bombing. You'd better prepare to see some gruesome scenes of death and destruction, Nelda. I guess when the Monitors hit, they hit hard."

"It looks as though a big rectangle has just been squashed flat—and over there—"

"Sure, the horrors of war. All the more reason for us to do our best to rally some organized opposition. Now relax for a few minutes, and let me pick a spot to sneak in."

The *Poopsie* whiffled low over a gaping break in the barrier of warehouses and piers, settled in behind a cluster of billboards. Blondel extricated himself from the pilot's seat with a sigh of relief, stretched cramped legs, then helped pry Nelda loose. Together they risked a look from behind their shelter. From somewhere, the cheery tones of Happy Horinip's voice echoed across the unheeding landscape.

"Good Lord," Blondel muttered. "Acres—square miles, maybe—level as a pool table."

"Look over there!" Nelda pointed. Dim in the pearly morning gloom, a tall, many-spired tower rose behind a surviving huddle of gas stations and hot-dog stands.

"Ye Gods!" Blondel hissed. "Instant skyscrapers!"

"They've—they've practically wiped out the city!" Nelda gasped. "I'd hardly know the place—my own home town!"

"I guess Blackwish was right," Blondel said grimly. "Saturation bombing."

"Still, it's odd the destruction is so sort of orderly," Nelda said.

"Sure, they've already bulldozed the wreckage. Probably didn't even wait to rescue the survivors."

"The monsters!"

"Let's get moving," Blondel urged. "We've got things to do; every minute counts."

"Just a minute." Nelda pulled a zipper, wriggled out of her arctic gear to reveal a zebra-striped leotard, a coral pink peasant blouse, and a chartreuse leather jacket with copper rivets, a major general's stars, and tassels on the breast pockets.

"That's, uh, quite an outfit," Blondel commented.

"Kind of conventional, I know," Nelda confessed. "But I felt I ought to dress inconspicuously, under the circumstances."

"Good thinking."

They crossed a vacant lot, started along a narrow street leading up through a gloomy canyon of soot-blackened masonry which ended at a clean-swept expanse of bare earth.

"I wonder where all the dead bodies and rubble are?" Nelda wondered.

"Blasted clean," Blondel marveled. "Looks like the Bonneville Salt Flats."

"Funny how it left the buildings right next to it standing."

"Shaped charges," Blondel explained.

"Listen!" Nelda plucked at his sleeve. "What's that?

"Sounds like the El is still running."

They followed the sound, two blocks east came upon a ramshackle construction of rusted iron and grimed brick, apparently held together by tattered posters announcing the joys of Fast, Efficient Rail Service. A string of ancient coaches with the raffish look of drunken sailors surprised by dawn waited, doors open as invitingly as fresh-dug graves.

"How about it?" Blondel inquired doubtfully.

"I'm game," Nelda said. "After all, spies have to take chances."

They selected seats in a car reminiscent of the James Boys' heyday, looked over the truss and toupé ads. A thin, seamed man with a narrow crooked head and a thatch of bristly tan hair under a cloth cap appeared from the shadows at the far end of the car, sidled closer.

"You folks been married long?" he inquired.

"No," Blondel said shortly.

"We're not married." Nelda sniffed.

"Tsk," said the small man.

"Say, when did the Monitors hit the town?" Blondel inquired. "Many people killed? What's the Air Force doing about it?"

"I don't pay no attention to that stuff," the man said mildly. "You folks wouldn't happen to have a bottle of wine on you, would you?"

"No. What are these buildings they're putting up?"

"Beats me. You know they closed down every bar in town? Man can't even drop in for a little refreshing sip of something."

"Have they taken hostages?"

"Milk. They're giving it away. Federal men, hah! I tell you, if this kind of creeping socialism goes on—"

"Federal men? You mean we've hit back, taken the city back from them?" Blondel asked excitedly.

"These G Men in the yella suits," the man explained. "All over like Salvation Army lassies at a race track. Man can't even get hold of a good bottle of Port."

"They're not government men," Blondel said. "They're foreigners."

". . . I mean, you take wine. Good, and good for ye." The little man swung closer to Blondel, bumped him lightly. "Well, so long, folks—"

"Hey," Nelda yipped. "That little creep took something out of your pocket."

Blondel patted himself, frowned. The little man grinned sheepishly and produced a folded packet of papers.

"You know, a feller can't work under these here conditions," he said sheepishly, handing them back. "That's these Federal men for ye, take a man's living right out from under him."

"You've got a nerve," Nelda stated.

"Takes a good set of nerves, honey," the man said nodding. "Man spends years learning a trade, and these boys hit town and put him out of business. . . ."

"Stand over there," Blondel directed. "And keep your hands in sight."

"Been a crowd, the little lady never would of saw me," the man said sadly. "But these here new rules—everybody running here, running there, Federal men all over the place. You know a man can't even slip into a bar for a little sip of Muscatel—"

"Where is everybody?" Nelda asked plaintively. "Have they killed them all?"

The little man spoke behind his hand: "Brother, you ought to think about making a honest woman out of the little lady." He clacked his plates, looking Nelda over. "Purty little piece like that."

"The little lady asked a question," Blondel barked.

"Why, don't be rude," Nelda cooed, turning slightly to display her chest to better advantage. "I'm sure this nice man just didn't hear me."

"They're making 'em all go in for some kind of tests," the dip confided. "Me, I slipped away. Never did like them tests. I mean, who is this Kraut, Wassermann, anyway, he's so smart?"

"Is there any organized resistance?" Blondel persisted.

"Well, I get off here." The pickpocket sidled past Blondel. "Nice to of met ye, I'm sure." He leaned closer to Blondel, who clapped his hands over his pockets. "Just slip into a church and pray, brother. You'll see the light."

" 'By, now," Nelda trilled.

"It says right in the Bible, 'Take a little wine for thy stomach's sake, and for thine ofttimes infirmities,' " the man announced as he passed on along the car.

"Well, it looks as though he's taking the invasion calmly," Blondel said disgustedly. "I guess the booze has rotted his brain."

"Why, I thought he was a sweet little man," Nelda countered.

They rode on in silence for another quarter hour, dismounted at a station ringed in by still-standing structures. There were half a dozen Monitors in view.

"No blimps in sight," Blondel noted. "I guess they've gone back for another load." They proceeded to the street.

"My God." Nelda prodded his arm. "They're everywhere."

Blondel glumly surveyed the early-morning scene. The scattering of pedestrians was almost outnumbered by trim, gold-uniformed Monitors briskly directing the sparse traffic, retrieving kites from power lines, minding baby buggies, nodding and smiling at the passersby.

"They act as though they owned the place," Blondel muttered. "And these boobs seem to like the idea."

"Diabolically clever," Nelda nodded. "They've already insinuated themselves into the dependency pattern of the masses."

In the next block, Blondel paused to watch a pair of yellow-painted machines at work in a vacant block ringed with stark structures whose naked brickwork had been exposed by the removal of their neighbors. The egg-shaped vehicles, painted a bright yellow, rode easily a foot above the sea of broken rubble, sucking up a steady stream of shattered brick as cleanly as a vacuum cleaner removing spilled Wheaties from a rug, and disgorging stacks of glossy white discs in neat rows.

An elderly man standing by observing the process gave a shake of the head and spat. "Beats hell how them things chew bricks and sh—" His eye lit on Nelda. ". . . and, uh, excrete dinner plates," he finished. "Nice morning, ma'am." He ducked his head and sidled closer to Blondel.

"You can pick 'em, son," he stated solemnly from the corner of his mouth. "Give me a well-fleshed gal every time."

"What's that thing?" Blondel pointed to a long, low, yellow-painted vehicle of strange design approaching along the street. Through its clear plastic top and sides a row of passengers were visible, staring vacantly out at the view as the bus slid past, riding, like the dozers, on an air cushion.

"Bus," the old man stated. "Yep, I recollect one time in Kansas City—"

"The Monitors are operating a bus service?"

"Sure. Reckon somebody's got to—"

"What happened to the old ones?"

"Junked 'em, I s'pose. Ever been in Kansas City, son? There was this bar—"

"The cars—where are they?" Blondel looked around, noting for the first time the virtual absence of auto traffic.

"What cars was them, son?" the old man said absently. "Like I says, I was having a couple of quick ones, in this here bar, and—"

"The cars! The Buicks and Ramblers and Chevies!"

"Oh, them. Take a bus. Quicker and cheaper. Anyway, cars is outlawed. So I was setting on the stool, sipping a rye and water, and this—"

"Against the law?" Blondel queried.

"Not in Kansas City, son. A wide-open town. Booze, women, gambling—you name it—"

"How about dirty postcards?" Nelda interposed, and gave Blondel's arm a jerk. "Tell that old pimp to get lost."

"You got me wrong, lady!" the oldster protested. "I was jest—"

"But doesn't anybody care?"

"Not if you got a bankroll, son. Anyhow, there I was, rolling that smooth stuff around on my tongue, and this gal eases up beside me. Well, hell—"

"Blondel, you come along this instant, or I'm going straight to the police!" Nelda announced.

"I mean about the cars!" Blondel amplified.

The oldster looked sharply in both directions. "I don't see 'em. Where?"

"I *am*," Nelda said. "Just watch me."

"Nowhere," Blondel said. "That's the point! They talk about how they're bringing freedom, and the first thing they do is clamp down on private travel!"

"She tipped the scale at three hundred if it was a ounce." The old fellow gazed back down the golden years. "Alice, that was her name. Alice of Dallas."

"Police!" Nelda yelped.

"Where?" Blondel whirled, prepared to sprint for it. The old man held up a veined hand. "No harm intended, folks," he quavered. "Anyways, I ain't one of them child-molesters." He moved off quickly.

"What did you yell for?" Blondel demanded.

"You men," Nelda dismissed the gender with a daintily lifted lip. "All you think about is just one thing."

"That reminds me," Blondel snapped his fingers. "We forgot to eat our lunch."

In the next block, Nelda plucked at Blondel's sleeve and pointed at a surgical-green front crowded between a shabby Army store and a dubious-looking pool parlor.

"That looks like a quiet little restaurant. Let's go there."

"It looks like a do-it-yourself morgue," Blondel protested. "I had in mind one of those little places with a beam ceiling and a big copperbound beer-barrel back of the bar, where you can get a superbly grilled steak and a dandy little red wine for about a dollar and a quarter."

"Hunger must have driven you mad. Come on."

Wide, featureless doors swung open as they came up, causing an unshaven passerby to shy violently and quicken his pace. Inside, neat white-topped tables, all vacant, were ranged in orderly rows under ceiling strips which shed a dazzling glare below. They picked a spot near the door and looked around for a waiter.

"No wonder the place is deserted," Blondel said. "Rotten service."

"Good morning, sir, madam," a well-modulated voice said at his elbow. "May I suggest a blend of natural fruit and vegetables juices, fortified with appropriate minerals and biomins?"

Blondel jumped and swivelled his head to see a tall well-muscled youth in a neat yellow cutaway standing by, a napkin over his left arm, a look of alertly pleasurable anticipation on his well-chiseled features.

"Don't sneak up on me like that," Blondel barked. "For a minute I thought—"

"Why, Blondel, don't be so uncouth." Nelda smiled warmly at the waiter. "I'm sure the salad will be perfectly lovely."

The waiter inclined his head. "Surely, madam." He plucked a small silvery tube from his breast pocket, held out a hand to her. "May I?" he murmured.

"Why—you dear man." Nelda put her plump hand in his. "I never saw any sense in these artificial social distinct—ow!" She jerked her hand back and sucked at the base of her thumb. "Blondel!" she said around it. "He stung me!"

"Madam! A thousand pardons!" The waiter looked distressed, staring at the tube he had touched to Nelda's hand. "My metabolic assessor must be out of adjustment." He shook it, frowned at it, then turned an expression of deep concern on the girl.

"My dear young lady," he said in a grave tone. "It's fortunate you dropped in when you did. Were you aware that you suffer from a number of dangerous physiochemical imbalances, any one of which might have resulted in permanent somatic damage?"

"I am?" Nelda took her thumb out of her mouth.

The waiter turned to Blondel. "The left hand, please, sir—just in case you're in even worse shape than the young lady."

"I don't want my fortune told," Blondel said shortly. "Just give me a menu."

"Oh, there's no need of that, sir—"

"Right. I already know what I want. I'll have a sixteen ounce top sirloin, rare, cauliflower with a cheese sauce, a baked potato with sour cream, and a half bottle of a nice little Beaujolais—a '57 will do."

"For breakfast?" Nelda's expression was respectful.

"What do you mean, breakfast? This is last night's dinner."

"I regret, sir, that the items you mention aren't recommended for you. Suppose I just make a correct selection of highly nutritive mineral jellies and vitamin pastes—"

Blondel shook his head. "Don't bother pushing the specialty of the house. I know what I want. If you're out of sirloin, make it a fillet—if it's not too expensive."

"Oh, our comestibles are all free of charge, of course, sir," the waiter assured him. "But I'm afraid your knowledge of nutrition is deficient. You see—"

"Skip the personal cracks, Jack, and fetch me a steak—any cut!" Blondel barked. "And—" he paused and looked startled. "Did you say free of charge?"

"Of course, sir. One of the basic responsibilities of Government is the provision of food, clothing, and shelter to all citizens."

Blondel made a choking noise.

"Are you ill, sir?" the waiter inquired solicitously.

"This place—it's run by . . . by Monitors?"

"Of course, sir. One of our first acts was to remove all waiters from duty, as public menaces."

"I'm with you so far. What did you do to them, boil them in oil, or just hang them?"

"Hardly anything so drastic, sir. They were tested and assigned to duties more in consonance with their natural aptitudes. Many of them are doing nicely now as agricultural assistants, specializing in porciculture."

"Porky culture?" Nelda repeated.

"Slopping pigs," Blondel explained. "Well, that's understandable. But now, as long as I'm here, how about rustling up my dinner, if you don't mind."

"You'd like the nutritive jelly?"

"Maybe we'd better have the old waiters back," Blondel said. "At least they gave you meat when you asked for it, if it was only a thumb in the soup."

"Do you really insist on this unwise selection, sir? Animal flesh is not the proper ration for you, biochemically speaking."

"Jelly isn't the proper ration, psychologically speaking. Better get me the steak before I take a bite out of a Monitor."

"Hmmm." The Monitor looked thoughtful. "The psychological aspect may have been inadequately considered by our dietetic engineers, which *could* account for the lack of response to our announcements of the new free food facilities." He waved a hand at the empty hall.

"You know, on second thought, I'd better consider *my* psyche, too," Nelda spoke up decisively. "Skip the juice and bring me a nice baked squab—make it two—and one of those cute little French omelettes. Just a small one—about six eggs; and don't bother putting anything much in it—just some onion, ham, endives, pimento, and maybe just a sprinkling of mushrooms—the little gray ones, please. And some coffee. And maybe a few buckwheat cakes to keep me occupied while you roll the main dish."

"Madam! Let me urge you to reconsider—"

"Bring it *now!*" Blondel ordered sternly. "Or your customer load may drop off to nothing again."

"Oh, don't go, sir!" The waiter hurried away.

"We ought to get out of here, fast, while he's not looking," Blondel said. "But I'm too weak to move."

"My God," Nelda said. "Wasn't that the cutest waiter? I hope he remembers to bring real maple syrup, instead of one of those ghastly apricot-flavored synthetics."

Blondel looked around at the sterile-looking dining room. "If this is the best they can do, the masses will uprise to throw out the invader before I can get them organized."

"Humph," Nelda said. "I get the distinct impression the exploited masses are sinking into an even deeper apathy than usual. If we don't succeed in convincing these Monitors they're not wanted, immediately, it may be too late."

Blondel chewed the inside of his lip. "I promised the general I'd pass his message on to his Underground Unit here in Chicago. We'll have to attend to that first."

Blondel drew out the packet of instructions Blackwish had passed to him, broke the seal, released the elastic band and folded back the first sheet. Below a line of excited red print stating the penalties for unauthorized use, an address caught his eye.

"Where's South Nixon Avenue?"

Nelda shrugged. "Who cares?"

"We have to find it before we can get on to our rebellion-fomenting," Blondel pointed out.

"Hah! *I* didn't promise Blockwits I'd do his dirty spying for him!" Nelda declared. "Just as soon as I've had my little breakfast I'm going to walk right up to the first Monitor I see and tell them to leave!"

"Uh—Nelda. Don't you think maybe you should just write an anonymous letter? For the present, we're OK, as long as they don't recognize us. But if you come right out and tell them you don't like them, they may take you away and operate on that undernourished psyche of yours."

"Sir, you can rest assured that no citizen

will be molested for expressing his views."
The waiter deftly slipped a laden tray before Nelda.

"Damn it, don't creep around like that!"
Blondel bellowed. "You're tying my nerves into Austrian knots!" He stuffed the papers hastily back into an inner pocket.

"Sorry, sorry, sir. I shall try to approach more noisily next time."

"Blondel, you apologize this instant!"
Nelda commanded.

"Hah! You were the one who was going to tell him you didn't want his kind around, and that they should all go back where they came from!"

"Why, the nerve!"

"I hope you'll find the steak savory, sir,"
the waiter interjected blandly, as he placed Blondel's tray before him. Blondel opened his mouth to reply, sniffed, picked up his knife and fork and sawed off a large bite of beef. It was crusty black on the outside, pale pink and juicy at the center. He closed his eyes and chewed. A contented expression appeared on his face.

"Adequate," he said. "Now go away and don't come around again until I call you."

"Yes, sir." The Monitor disappeared. Nelda glared at Blondel. "I'm beginning to see you as you really are, Blondel! You're as reactionary as old Blockwits, in your own sneaky way! You actually harbor the medieval idea that a cute man like that waiter is your inferior merely because he's engaged in one of the service professions!"

"Um," Blondel said, chewing.

"I wouldn't be surprised to learn that your ostensibly superior attitude actually screens a deep sense of inadequacy, brought on by a suppressed resentment of his tremendous physical attractiveness!"

"If you're not going to eat those crackers, could I have them?"

"This same type of sublimation of unacceptable animalistic impulses is at the bottom of a great portion of the world's ills, I'll bet."

"Hurry up and eat. We have to get away from here before he realizes who I am."

"What's your hurry? I'm thinking of giving him my telephone number, just in case he needs someone to turn to, or something."

"Swell. Only you don't have a phone number. Besides which, I thought we were a couple of undercover agents."

"Don't imagine that any sympathy one individual may have aroused by his obvious personal *simpatico* in any way influences my total ideological opposition to the concept of authoritarian government!"

"The thought never entered my head."

"You needn't try to dragoon *me* into your schemes! I told you—"

"You told me you were going to give your pitch to the Monitors. OK, here's your chance. Just tell the waiter your views. I'll wait outside."

Nelda was shaking her head stubbornly. "I'd be simply too, too embarrassed, after your boorish behavior."

Blondel speared the last bit of steak, pushed back his chair. "In that case let's get out of here quick, before he comes back."

"What about the bill?"

"It's free; you heard him."

"Aren't you even going to leave a tip?"

"What's ten per cent of nothing? Anyway, I didn't think you approved of such class-conscious gestures."

"Well—it seems terribly abrupt. . . ." She rose, emitted a small, ladylike burp.

"He's probably out calling in a strong-arm squad," Blondel guessed. "Come on . . ."

They hurried quietly across to the entry vestibule, paused to peer out into the street.

"I trust you found everything satisfactory, sir, and madam," an eager-to-please voice sounded in Blondel's ear. The waiter, in regulation Monitorial yellows, caught the door as it swung open and gave him an encouraging smile.

"Oh, it was divine," Nelda cooed. "And your attentiveness made it ever so much better."

"Somebody needs to hang a bell on you," Blondel stated hotly. "My pulse has been leaping like a gazelle at five minute intervals ever since I came into this joint!"

"Pay no attention to my escort," Nelda said sweetly. "He suffers from a severe case of ingrown ego." She fluttered her large blue eyes at the Monitor and swept through the door, bumping both sides of the frame in passing. The Monitor ducked his head politely at Blondel.

"Sir, since I notice that you and the young lady are new arrivals here, perhaps I might volunteer my services in showing you some of the improvements that have been made in the last few days."

"Uh, no, we—" Blondel started.

"Why, how perfectly ducky!" Nelda trilled. "What a simply sweet suggestion, isn't it, Blondel?"

He turned to her, muttered: "We want to shake this creep, remember?"

"He can show us where to find that silly address you're looking for," she hissed, then gave the Monitor another burst from her eyelashes. "We'd be too thrilled for words, ah . . . what *is* your name, you darling thing?"

"Pekkerup, madam, at your service."

"How did you know we're new arrivals?" Blondel inquired as the trimly-built young man took up his station on Nelda's left.

"Your arrival was monitored, of course." Their guide raised a finger and a small yellow helicopter came whiffling down from somewhere above eye level, settled at the curb. The bubble canopy popped open. There was no pilot at the controls, Blondel noted.

"Just take seats," Pekkerup invited, "and—"

"We'll walk," Blondel stated firmly, backing away.

"As you wish." The Monitor waved again; the hatch slammed shut. The empty copter hopped straight up, flitted away over the rooftops.

"You boys have some pretty cute gadgets," Blondel said nervously.

"There are any number of useful devices we'll introduce in the near future," Pekkerup said. "For the present, we're limited to these rather clumsy machines which approximate the aboriginal level of mechanical complexity. We always feel it's important to avoid precipitating cultural shock, of course."

"Naturally."

"Now, suppose we stroll over to the new Avenue of Positive Thinking. It's just a square away, and it will give you a better idea of how the city will appear after the slum clearance is completed."

Blondel followed glumly as the Monitor led the way, with Nelda clinging to his arm and chattering gaily. They passed a block of unwashed display windows stacked with pawned revolvers, plastic secret agent outfits and artificial limbs, emerged abruptly at the edge of a broad expanse of immaculate green lawn on the far side of which a row of pastel-colored structures of fanciful design rose in an intricate pattern against the early morning sky.

"My God, what's happened to State Street?" Nelda blurted.

"Just a simple matter of removing the existing huts and installing structures more appropriate to the aesthetic sensitivities of the people," Pekkerup explained cheerfully.

"What do you call it, Miami Beach on the Runway?" Blondel inquired.

"Actually, the new name of the city is Sapphire," the Monitor said. "All the new nomenclature will be drawn from the existing cultural matrix—"

"What was wrong with Chicago?"

"The village, or the word itself?"

"Skip it. What's the idea of a grass street a hundred yards wide?"

"Oh, it isn't a street in the old sense. That is, it is not a raceway for individually-controlled personal vehicles. After the remainder of the plantings are in place, the people will find it a pleasant, shady walk on which to stroll about their business and contemplate the pleasing new façades."

"Swell. The people are going to love that a lot," Blondel stated.

"We thought so. The buildings themselves will house the various official agencies necessary for the opening stages of organization. Then, after the initial educational effort is complete, they will be made available to the public as housing for those who prefer to remain in a civic environment."

They crossed the wide avenue, empty except for a lone mongrel pup trotting along nose to pavement in pursuit of private canine interests. On the far side, a curbstone, embellished with carved foliage, edged a wide belt of flower beds set like jewelry displayed on green velvet. The buildings, each different from its neighbor in design, finish and tint, were placed at generous intervals, linked by walkways lined with still more blossoms. The trio paused before a fluted and corniced front of glossy pale purple, trimmed with pale orchid meanders.

"Why—I do believe those are shops," Nelda said eagerly, her eyes fixed on what were obviously display windows nestled back among the flowering shrubs flanking the wide ground level entrances.

"Yes, indeed," the Monitor agreed. "They stock artifacts appropriate to your present curious economy. I think you'll be pleased to see what the planet is capable of producing for your use when properly managed, even at its present low level of technological development."

Nelda rummaged in a capacious handbag which she had produced from somewhere. "My God, and me with only a dollar seventy-nine and an IRT token!"

"Old-fashioned currency will not be required, madam," the Monitor assured her. "Any debit incurred will be entered against your basic quotas."

"You mean—I can open charge accounts?"

"You might call it that—"

"I just *hate* shopping," Nelda said happily, "but there are a few little things I need. . . ."

Blondel trailed as Nelda forged to the van, shooting sharp glances at the goods in view. There were bright displays of cooking utensils, books, fishing tackle, furniture moulded of smooth plastic and upholstered in vivid hues. Blondel paused to admire a colorfully enameled auto chassis of unfamiliar design, featuring individual power to each of the four wheels, and what appeared to be retractable flotation gear.

He looked up at a yelp from Nelda. "A dress shop! My God, I hope they have something cute for the well-filled-out girl!"

"Yes indeed; provision has been made for deformed individuals of all types," Pekkerup stated. "Of course, as soon as the nutrition programs have had time to produce their results, such measures will be unnecessary."

"Luckily for you, she's in a trance," Blondel advised the Monitor as they followed Nelda up the broad steps and through a door into a cheerfully-lit interior lavishly decorated with displays of gay-colored clothes.

"My God! What a perfectly darling Hooshkah!" Nelda grabbed a voluminous garment from a display rack and held it at arm's length. "With a sweet little reverse-pleated bodice, and that exquisite Empress Agatha hemline!"

"What is she saying?" The Monitor looked inquiringly at Blondel.

"Who knows?" He went past her, through an arch, and into a second sales room, where display cases exhibited polished and enameled assemblies of metal, variously equipped with moving parts, cutting edges, instruction labels, and self-contained motive power.

"Wow!" Blondel reached for a shiny unit the size of a grapefruit, painted a bright hue, with chrome-plated levers and bolt-heads. It was satisfyingly heavy.

"It's a beauty!" he stated. "What is it?"

"A hobbyist's multipurpose shaper," an alert voice said behind him. Blondel leaped, almost dropped the shaper.

"For the more advanced enthusiast, we have the Home Shop model." The clerk, a handsomely-built young fellow in tailored yellow coveralls pointed to a slightly larger gadget, this one bright red. "And then, of course, there is the professional model with extra-high capacity, air bearings, a thousand MT power unit, and self-honing edges." Blondel admired the bulky bright orange machine, moved on to the next table as a yelp of pleasure sounded from Nelda in the shop next door.

"Say, those are dandy-looking jobs. . . ." He gazed hungrily at a row of banana-sized green-bodied machines with milled fittings and large shiny push buttons.

"Yes, sir, we feel that our line of fully internally-grounded auto-tuning grablifiers answers a long-felt need."

"You bet." Blondel ran his fingers lovingly over the sleek surface, noting the micrometer scale, the conveniently-placed on-and-off button, the tiny red and green indicator lights. "Uh . . . what does it do?"

"There's nothing like it for tuning an extranial culminator—and for many other uses, as well." From the dress shop, another shrill cry of delight rang.

Blondel passed on to the next rack where recognizable hand tools, roller skates, flashlights, and microscopes were displayed among highly-polished marine clocks and beautifully machined miniature lathes.

"Perhaps you'd like to try one of our personalized earplug tape players," the clerk suggested. "Weighs two grams and plays nine hours of your favorite music without changing settings."

"I'm tone deaf," Blondel resisted, sidestepping the salesman and heading for a row of iridescent pink, blue, green, puce, and magenta motorcycles as another cry of joy sounded from next door.

"You might wish to try one of our seatpack roto flyers," the clerk persisted, pointing out a display of bright-plated six-foot rods attached to padded plastic saddles and topped by counter-rotating three-foot blades. "A boon to the footsore, and a source of pleasure to those who long to soar solitary among the clouds."

Blondel wiped the moisture from his chin, let his dazzled eyes roam across the massed hardware as the salesclerk patted the sleek prow of a powerboat.

"What about a nice little twelve-foot, two-hundred horsepower, noncapsizing, directionally-stable, leak-proof—"

"No." Blondel took a deep breath, squeezed his eyes shut, and turned, blundered back across the store and into the neighboring emporium, where Nelda stood picking over an assortment of gossamer superfluities.

"Get hold of yourself," he said shakily. "I know it's a great temptation, but we can't start trafficking with the enemy."

"Never mind the sermon." Nelda wrinkled her nose. "They didn't have anything I liked."

"Suppose I take you along to see the new Universal Enlightenment Center," Pekkerup proposed. "The Individual Potential testing program is in full swing there now. Within the next four days, we expect to have processed the entire population of Sapphire, and be ready to commence the retraining phase."

"Thanks a lot," Blondel said, "but I guess we've got to be scooting along now. . . ."

"Don't be silly." Nelda attached herself to Pekkerup's arm. "I'm absolutely fascinated by any kind of cultural stuff."

"We've, er, got a couple of errands to run, remember?" Blondel muttered to Nelda.

"Later," Nelda said complacently. "Let's go, Pecky."

"I'm sure you'll both be most interested in what we're doing at the Center," the guide predicted. "Our mission there is to discover the highest potentialities of each individual citizen, then to administer precisely that training which will enable him to realize those potentials, thus putting an end to the frightful waste of human capabilities."

"Oh, I don't know," Blondel protested.

"We already have pretty good methods of deciding who gets what job. I don't know any pilots who are quadruple amputees, and a blind man doesn't have much chance of landing a post as a color consultant—unless it's with the Civil Service, and—"

"Many of your potential nuclear physicists are laboring as copra cutters for lack of appropriate training," Pekkerup interrupted gently. "The responsible positions have traditionally gone to those persons with the loudest voices and the most resilient scruples. That situation no longer obtains."

As they talked, they had followed a winding path that curved between flowering shrubs to emerge at the edge of a ten-acre reflecting pool lined with white towers linked by airy walkways and flanked by broad, tree-dotted gardens.

"Ooooh." Nelda gripped Pekkerup's arm tighter. "I'd be petrified if I had to walk across one of those little bridges!"

"Not at all." The Monitor pointed, casually lifting the girl from her tiptoes. She yelped and let go. "I can assure you that with half an hour's reorientation you'll find yourself relieved of this and other neurotic compulsions."

"I'm not sure I'd like that." Nelda rubbed an elbow she had cracked against the Monitor's biceps.

"You'll find it most pleasant, Miss Monroe."

Nelda paused in mid-simper. "Gee," she said thoughtfully. "How did you know my name?"

"It's one of the functions of efficient government to be aware of what its citizens are about." Pekkerup smiled blandly at her. "Shall we go inside?" He indicated wide steps leading into the nearest of the palatial white structures.

Blondel looked around. There were half a dozen ordinary citizens of what had formerly been Chicago in sight, loitering around the edge of the pool or napping in the shade of the trees. The rest of the visible persons were Monitors, standing alertly in groups of twos or threes, or strolling casually along the walks.

"Nelda," he said. "It's time to go. We're keeping this fellow from his duties."

"Not at all." Pekkerup urged Nelda up the first of the steps. Blondel had the distinct impression that several more Monitors had turned casually toward them.

"Let's go." Blondel took her other arm and tugged. Nelda raised a sturdy foot and placed it against his stomach.

"Get lost," she suggested, and administered a hearty shove. Blondel staggered back, sat down abruptly. A pair of Monitors were definitely walking briskly toward them now. Nelda had turned her back and was tucking up a stray curl.

"Nelda!" Blondel yelled. "We have to get out of here before it's too late!"

"Some people just don't know when their advances have been rejected," she said loudly.

Blondel leaped up, dodged around Pekker-up, and sprinted for the cover of a clump of weeping willows.

CHAPTER EIGHT

After a brisk chase lasting half an hour, during which Blondel's well-developed instincts indicated pursuit close behind, he went to ground in a dim-lit chili and tequila house peopled by furtive persons of unmistakably non-Monitorial appearance.

"What's fer you, gringo?" a large man with thin reddish hair and pale blue eyes demanded when Blondel had settled himself in a rear booth with a view of the door.

"*Una cerveza, muy frio,*" Blondel specified.

"Huh?"

"*Pronto, por favor, amigo.*"

"Jist a minute. I better get one o' these greasers to translate. I don't savvy that wetback lingo."

"Never mind," Blondel said. "Just get me a beer."

The large man gave Blondel a suspicious look and went away. Moments later a shadow fell across his shoulder. He looked up. A tall preternaturally lean man, with a face like saddle leather and a patch over one eye, silently took the seat across from him.

"Uh ... *buenos dias*," Blondel said cautiously.

The newcomer shot a keen look at him, took a folded newspaper from his pocket and began to read.

S-v-e-n-s-k-a D-a-g-b-l-a-d-e-t, Blondel spelled out. The waiter returned with the beer; the stranger ignored him. He ignored the stranger. Blondel took a swallow. His mouth seemed drier than ever. He checked his pulse. It was still racing from the run. He cleared his throat.

"*Los Monitoros*," he began, "*esta usted ...*" The stranger shot him a piercing glance above the paper.

"*Förbannade Amerikanerna*," he said in a gravelly tone. "*Prata, prata, som en papegoja!*"

"*Förlåt*," Blondel muttered. "*Det var fel.*" He finished his beer hurriedly and rose. A leather-jacketed man seated at the bar caught his eye. He hesitated, then went over, took the stool beside him. The man leaned casually closer.

"Lefty send you?" he murmured.

"No."

The man pondered that. "Good," he said. "Never did trust that Lefty."

"Still," Blondel said on impulse, "maybe you could help me."

"Yeah?" the other said guardedly.

"Where's, ah, 2378½ South Nixon Avenue?"

"That in Chi?"

"Sure."

The dark man finished his drink—a murky, dark green fluid in an old-fashioned glass—and gave Blondel a quick look. "Got two bits?" he inquired from the corner of his mouth.

"Yeah," Blondel whispered back. He fished the coin from his pants pocket and handed it over. The man looked at it carefully, rose and started for the door.

"Hey! Where are you going with my quar—" Blondel caught himself as numerous sets of dark eyes as impassive as olive pits turned his way. He dropped a bill on the bar, halted at a growl from the bartender.

"That'll be a buck-fifty for the brew, gringo."

"Kind of high, isn't it?"

"It's imported."

"From where?"

"Jersey City."

"Oh." Blondel added a Kennedy half dollar to the bill and hurried after his new contact. Outside, he caught sight of him rounding a corner thirty feet distant. He ran for it, but the man had disappeared from view.

"Damn!" Blondel muttered, ducking under a string of nudie magazines festooned across the front of a modest stall. "It was my 1912 D, too. . . ." He turned back and collided with a man who gave him a warning look.

"Oh, there you are." Blondel fell silent as the man hooked a finger at the news vendor.

"Got a map of the city?" he muttered.

"Two bits." The vendor handed across a garishly-printed document. The man turned, poked it into Blondel's flaccid hand, and disappeared into the crowd.

"Wow, what an organization," Blondel murmured admiringly.

Half a block further, in a small park apparently devoted to wastepaper collection and pigeon culture, Blondel took a bench, scanned the brush for observers, then unfolded the map. Nixon Avenue was clearly marked as lying in square B-4.

At that moment a large bus of the old type thundered up, belching fumes. Blondel hurried to it, clambered aboard as it surged ahead.

"Does this bus go anywhere near B-4?" he asked the driver, a squatty, morose-looking man in a gray wind-breaker and a warped billcap.

"Before what, Jack? How's about moving back in the bus."

"I mean Nixon Avenue," Blondel corrected.

"East or West?"

"South," he said.

"Nope," the driver said.

"Nope what?"

"Nope it don't."

"It doesn't go to square B-4—I mean South Nixon?"

"Goes to East Nacton, that any help?"

"No," he said.

"No, what?"

"No, it isn't."

"Tough."

"What?"

"Skip it, Jack. Go sit down, OK?"

Muttering, Blondel found a seat between a large colored lady who was carrying on a spirited conversation with an unseen friend, and a lean white-haired little man who planted a rubber-tipped cane on Blondel's foot and exerted a surprising amount of pressure.

"Ah—would you mind, sir?" Blondel tried to extricate his foot.

"Mind what, buster?" The oldster clacked his plates at Blondel and indicated a multi-colored World War One Victory ribbon dangling from a curled lapel. "I took a Jerry 88 millimeter right through the gonads. I guess I got a few rights."

"Sure, but your cane—"

". . . and I says to that lady," the mutter on Blondel's right rose in volume, "back home ole Missy never mind a little totin; then *she* say . . ."

"When the call come, we was the ones went, but nowadays that don't mean dood-ley-squat, the way some people talk."

". . . so I say, way some peoples ack, seem

like they got some wrong notions bout who
runnin' this country . . ."

". . . was down to the VA just Monday a
week. Some young fairy in a purple necktie
tried to tell me what the law meant. Hell, I
was peeling spuds at Fort Bliss while he
was still on the tit!"

"My foot—"

The cane lifted momentarily and came
down hard. "I didn't get this here medal
reading no lawyers' fine print, I told him.
And . . ."

". . . and *she* say, she goin' call the police-
mens, and *I* say, I goin' call the NAAC of P,
and she say . . ."

"If you'd lift your cane, sir—"

". . . ain't my fault if I didn't happen to
come under fire, was it? I give up a swell
job in the A & P to go to war. and what I
say is . . ."

". . . and *I* say, how did I know the family
prefer the white meat, and *she* say her hus-
band say he done forgot a chicken had laigs,
been so long since he seen anything but
necks and backs, and *I* say . . ."

". . . ready to go to war tomorrow, if duty
calls! Sure, I got a little forty per cent
disability, but, hell, I always say a little
dose ain't no worse'n a bad cold!"

"Pardon me, Colonel, would you mind taking your cane off my foot?" Blondel inserted
the request in the cross fire.

"Sure, son. I'm getting off here." The old
fellow rose, leaning heavily on the cane.

The colored lady gestured, driving a large elbow in under Blondel's fifth rib. ". . . and I say, I guess I has no choice but to resign my position, and she say, 'But Pulchritude, how I goin' do without you,' and I say, 'I goin' miss them babies somethin' dreadful,' and she fix to cry, and I fix to cry—"

"So long, junior." The vet saluted Blondel. "Your fly's open."

By the time Blondel had investigated and found the remark groundless, the bus was again in motion.

"Mister." The dark lady leaned toward Blondel. "That old gemmun a bad influence; way he talk all the time a pusson can't hear herself think."

"Funny," Blondel said, "I could hear you clearly." He peered out the window, seeking to identify a landmark.

"You one them telempaths?" his neighbor inquired suspiciously.

"No, I'm a more of psychopath. Either that, or everyone else is."

"Ummm, ummm . . . you in a bad way," his new friend opined. "That one of the first signs."

"What about you?" Blondel wagged a finger. "Don't you care that the country's been invaded?"

"It *is*?"

"Of course! Who do you think knocked down half the city and ordered private vehicles off the streets and took over the radio and TV stations and fired the cops and,

and . . ." He waved a hand at a stretch of cleared ground the bus was passing. "And all the rest of it."

"I figure that them Republicans."

"The Monitors said over the radio they were taking over! They announced it publicly!"

"I never listens to them commercials; I is learned to just naturally tune 'em out."

Blondel waved a hand at his fellow passengers, slumped complacently in their seats. "I don't understand. You all act as though nothing had happened!"

The bus slowed, and the lady rose. "Trouble with you, you one dem radicals," she stated disapprovingly. "You needs to get together with Jesus and talk things over."

Blondel got hastily to his feet. "Say, I wonder if you could tell me which bus to catch for Nixon Avenue—" He broke off short and retreated to the back of the bus as two smiling young Monitors swung aboard the vehicle. From a new seat between a pair of glowering, bearded teen-agers, he observed the invaders as they exchanged familiar greetings with the driver, bypassed the fare box and took seats near the front.

For the next forty minutes Blondel sat pressed back unobtrusively in his seat, now burying himself in a newspaper picked up from the seat beside him, now pretending deep interest in the laxative ads above the windows after his concealment was abruptly reclaimed by its owner. The bus was al-

most empty by the time the yellow-clad pair
stood, sauntered to the rear door and looked
him over with friendly smiles, preparing to
descend. Blondel braced himself, belatedly remembering Blackwish's instructions regarding the documents he had entrusted to him.

The bus halted; the first Monitor stepped
down; the second nodded, said: "Nice morning, Mr. Blondel," and followed. Blondel
was still staring after them as the bus pulled
away from the curb.

Blondel left the bus at the next stop, a
bleak, windswept intersection fronted on one
side by the grim bulks of warehouses, on
the other by the desolation of railroad yards
behind which a single slender tower loomed
in evidence of Monitorial activity in the area.
A thin woman in a flimsy print dress above
knobby, nylon-clad knees gave him a specu-
lative look, detached herself from the lamp
post against which she had been leaning
and gave her brillo-like hair a pat.

"You looking for some action, sweetie?"
She had a voice like a cracked beer stein.

"I'm looking for Nixon Avenue."

"What's there, some o' them cut-rate
houses?"

"Just looking up a friend," Blondel reassured her. "You see, I got on the wrong bus
and—"

"Them damned amateurs are wrecking
the trade," the woman said sadly.

"Sure, but what I wanted to know was—"

" 'Course, you boys are always on the look-out for something free—"

"Oh." Blondel offered a dollar bill. The woman eyed it dubiously.

"May be some dollar stuff over there on Nixon Avenue, but around here it'll run you five, plus sales tax."

"Just for giving me directions?"

"Directions? You mean you need lessons?"

"I want to know where Nixon Avenue is!"

"Back to that, huh? Well, there ain't nothing they can teach you over there you can't learn quicker right here, honey."

"You mean—you're . . . ah . . . ?"

"Let your hair down, sugar. I'm a professional, go ahead and say it."

"Amazing," Blondel shook his head. "Blackwish must have a better organization than J. Edgar Hoover."

She backed away. "Now, hold on, brother, let's leave them boys out of this."

"I guess you're right; discretion pays." Blondel lowered his voice. "But the point is, I have a message to deliver. They're holding him—"

"Who?"

"You think I should mention his name?"

"Suit yourself. Holding him where?"

"In the house, of course."

"It figures. But why come to me? A independent ain't got a chance up against the big chains."

"He says they're watching every move he makes."

"One o' *them* kind of places, hey?"

"They've got him outnumbered about twenty to one, of course."

"The poor feller." She clucked in sympathy.

"And he thought maybe you—"

"Not me. One trick at a time, that's what mother taught her girls."

"But if you got a few men together—you know, rugged types . . ."

"I don't like the sound o' that, feller," the woman said severely.

". . . you could all sneak into the woodshed and come up in his bedroom."

"You can have your buck back, mister. That ain't my kind of party." She turned and retreated hastily around the corner.

"Everybody in SCRAG is out of his or her mind," Blondel complained aloud. He looked around, spotted a faded street sign dangling under a shattered luminaire. Half a minute's research with his map indicated that he was now two and one-quarter inches north northeast of the 2000 block of South Nixon. He tightened his belt and set out on foot.

The sun was low above the city's oddly punctuated skyline when Blondel, after half a dozen narrow escapes from Monitor patrols, dodged past the last knot of idlers, took a short-cut through an alley and emerged on the home stretch. Nixon Avenue, the map indicated, lay just beyond the next open expanse which reached to a belt of newly placed trees, incongruous in the aroma of stockyard wafted by the evening breeze:

For the moment there were no Monitors in view. Blondel, wincing at the pain in his blistered feet, skirted the cleared acreage, keeping in the deepening shadows of the tottering structures which ringed it.

Taking his bearings on an illuminated green minaret towering in the distance, he entered a gap in the hedge, ducking under boughs heavy with night-blooming flowers. Shortly thereafter he made the discovery that the blossoms were accompanied by thorns. After a short pause, during which he turned up his coat collar and wrapped his hands in handkerchiefs, he pressed on.

It was a difficult quarter hour in the thorn bushes. But at the end lights showed, glowing dimly ahead. Flat on the ground now, Blondel wriggled under a last set of barbs, poked his head out into the clear. Across a wide lawn, the dark shapes of lacy buildings loomed, sparkling with tiny lights that glowed on balconies, towers, aerial walkways—

"My God, Blondel!" a familiar voice yapped from close at hand. "Are you still skulking around here?"

Sitting morosely on the far end of the marble bench occupied by Nelda, now clad in a flowing robe of gossamer white, Blondel massaged his feet.

"I did *not* come here to beg for a second

chance," he stated firmly. "As a matter of fact, I thought Nixon Avenue was somewhere around here."

"It was," Nelda said carelessly. "They removed it to make room for the Aspiration Building."

"Great! Why didn't you tell me that this morning?"

"I had other things on my mind." She gave him a disapproving look. "Where have *you* been all day?"

"Making valuable contacts," he said shortly. "But I still have the problem of delivering the general's distress call."

"I suggest you take it and sho—"

"Ah, there you are, dear lady," a smooth voice called. Blondel stared through the gloom at a yellow-clad figure approaching through the dusk.

"I'm too tired to run any more," Blondel groaned. "I'll stall him while you make your escape."

"Don't talk like a complete cretin, Blondel. I've changed my mind about the Monitors—"

"You don't understand, Nelda! You didn't kick me in the belly today because you wanted to; they took over your muscles and made you do it! Now's your chance to make a run for it!"

"Why, Pecky, you dear!" Nelda crooned. "Were you looking for me?"

"Yes—and Mr. Blondel!" The Monitor's face lighted as he saw the latter. "Miss Monroe and I are about to run over to our evening orientation session; won't you join us, Mr. Blondel?"

"Come on," Nelda urged. "You can't go running around rabble-rousing forever."

"I thought we agreed about the necessity for certain, er, measures," Blondel said guardedly.

"Thank heavens I've thrown off conventionalized thinking, and perceived the necessity for externalization of our societal mechanisms!" Nelda declared.

"Is that what they call defecting to the enemy?"

"Please, sir, cease regarding us as enemies . . ."

"You've been hounding me from one hiding place to another all day," Blondel retorted. "I don't call that evidence of friendly intentions."

"Oh?" Pekkerup seemed to confer briefly with unseen voices. "Ah, yes," he said. "You *were* an elusive chap today. . . ." Footsteps sounded, closing in along the walk. Blondel sat listlessly, waiting for the inevitable. A Monitor, indistinguishable from Pekkerup in the fading light, hove into view.

"Here you are, sir." He handed over a bundle of folded papers. "You dropped these here this morning. Sorry about the delay in returning them, but you seem to have a knack for dropping out of sight from time to time."

Blondel patted his pockets hastily, then

accepted the offering. "My laundry list," he explained lamely.

"Why not come along with me, sir?" the newcomer suggested. "I'm about to conduct a little question and answer period for a small group of citizens who've expressed special interest in the new programs."

"Will I get to sit down?"

"Of course—and refreshments will be served."

"It's a deal—but I'm not making any promises."

"Excellent, sir." The Monitor led Blondel, hobbling painfully, along a walk past a lantern-hung terrace, up broad steps and into a cosy amphitheater where half a dozen men in shabby garments sat huddled in a tight cluster in the far corner.

"Let's all gather round the table here," the Monitor called gaily, indicating a polished board surrounded by soft leather chairs. Blondel sank into one with a groan. A thin fellow in a worn turtle-neck slid into place on his right. A stolid thug, with hands like catcher's mitts projecting from an undersized pin stripe, creaked the chair on the left.

"Where's the eats?" the latter growled.

"Yes," Blondel echoed. "Where are the eats?"

The heavyweight cocked a scarred eyebrow at him. "Wisenheimer?" he inquired.

"Knackwurst," Blondel retorted.

His interrogator subsided, baffled. The Monitor was looking over his charges brightly.

"Gentlemen, the Tersh Jetterax recognizes that the little problem of communication of ideas lies at the bottom of the somewhat, ah, cool reception we Monitors have received among you. It is our hope, in little, informal, voluntary gatherings like this one, to put your minds at ease as to the ethical basis for the many improvements which are now being made in your lives. Who would like to lead off the discussion?"

"What about dames?" a grizzled man with one ear rumbled.

"Alas, no ladies chose to join us this evening."

"Don't rib me, bo. You said if I come, there'd be some kicks."

"Dames is poison," another veteran of life on a hostile planet offered. "No dames, I say. Cards, dice, ponies, plenty booze—that's fer me."

"Likker'll rot yer insides," a small, peppery derelict predicted. "You boys need to get on some good stuff." He winked a fluttery wink which triggered a tic in his left cheek which occupied his attention for the remainder of the session.

"Where's the eats?" the big man demanded loudly.

"Yes, where are the eats?" Blondel echoed.

"Gentlemen, the food will be served presently," the Monitor soothed. "First, let us deal with the problem uppermost in all our minds." He looked at a round-shouldered youth with pale stubble and a slack jaw who had so far not spoken. "You, sir: What troubles you, with reference to our presence among you?"

The youth stirred. His mouth closed and opened. "Huh?" he managed.

"Can you state what, precisely, interposes itself between you and a rational acceptance of your good fortune?"

"I got like a low IQ," the lad stated positively. He bobbed his head and grinned briefly, exposing wide-spaced teeth and a pink cud of bubble gum.

"Be of good cheer! As soon as your testing is complete you'll be trained for work well within your capabilities—"

"Nope," the youth stated flatly.

"What he needs," the peppery man declared, "is a stiff jolt right in the carotid. Fixes 'em every time."

"Where's the eats?"

"You give me the dames, you keep the booze."

"Surely you prefer productive work at a useful occupation to a drone's existence?" the Monitor inquired patiently.

"Nope."

"Doesn't the prospect of a spacious new apartment, comfortable and attractive clothing, improved health, greater intellectual vigor, and a meaningful role in the world's affairs attract you?"

"Nope."

"Hey! He's going to try to make us take some kind of bath," the little fellow on Blondel's right predicted. "And prob'ly preaching afterwards."

"I don't need no pansy in yeller britches telling me when to bathe off," the hungry one announced. "Where's the eats?"

"Surely you're excited by the prospect of participation in the great things happening about you today!" The Monitor radiated enthusiasm. "Picture it! A continent-wide program of landscape improvement which will convert the wilderness into parks and gardens! The deserts will be irrigated, new lands opened up for settlement, and new bright houses for all! In place of the clusters of dreary, unsightly constructions in which you've been crowded like beasts, radiant towers will rise among the lawns! The natural resources will be identified and put to use, power will be supplied free, from nuclear, tidal, and solar sources! All drudgery will be automated, and underground factories will produce endless streams of the goods required to make life more joyous! New highway systems, twenty lanes wide, one way, will link all major centers, and on them, improved, fail-proof vehicles will cruise at incredible speeds in perfect safety! A subsurface vacuum tube system will speed heavy cargo from coast to coast! Every citizen will thrill to new-found abilities at sports, sciences, the arts! Official programs of achievement in every field of human activity will uncover and develop every hidden talent; and the vast, untapped reservoir of genius latent in the undiscovered masses will be opened, freed to produce new symphonies, new sculptures, new formulae, new recipes, for the delight of all!''

"If you guys don't want the dames," the girl-fancier proposed, "I'll take 'em."

"Where's the eats?"

"Heck, a little horse don't hurt a man none—and that pot, why that's downright beneficial!"

"Yep, it's the old soap-and-salvation pitch," the anti-ablution man rose. "I knew it soon's I seen them brand-new store clothes he was wearing." He departed, muttering.

"Gentlemen, are your imaginations not fired by the prospect?" the Monitor called over the rising tide of comment.

"Nope," the dull youth stated.

"But—what *does* arouse your enthusiasm?" the Monitor appealed. "Surely there are ideals that move you more than the mere satisfaction of bodily hungers!"

"I like cars," the slack-jawed lad stated.

"Now you take snow, cut fifty to one . . ."

"Redheads—and blondes, and maybe a few black-headed ones, too—"

"But I can't get no driver's license."

"Boy, I can almost feel the old ten cc slipping in now," the addict said dreamily.

"I knew one dame was white-headed, premature. But don't kid yourself, Bub, her axles was greased . . ."

"So I got a couple chasses without no wheels set up in the side yard."

"Sirs! The discussion is wandering far afield! I'm here to put your minds at ease—"

"If there ain't no eats, I'm dusting." The large man got to his feet.

"Let's skip the chin-music and get on with the cure." The narcotics fan rubbed horny hands together. "Let me tell you, I tapered off in some o' the best sanitariums in the country. My niece—"

"What I say is, baths is OK, if they got dames to scrub yer back, like in Japan. I seen this here movie—"

"Gentlemen—"

"Pa likes refrigerators. He's got twelve of 'em out back."

"Ain't no action here, I can see that," the sport declared. "Maybe if I hustle I can get me a bolita ticket before Manny closes down fer the evening." He exited hurriedly.

"How about it, you going to let me down easy?" the junky called, still fighting the tic. "If you're reneging, speak up. I'm overdue for my fix."

"You know, I ain't seen a dame since I hit this joint," the one-eared man said in a tone of dawning comprehension. "I think this is one of them homo joints!" He got to his feet and stamped out of the hall. The Monitor darted back and forth in agitation.

"Please, gentlemen, don't go—"

"Never mind them," Blondel advised him. "I wanted to ask you—"

"Come back!" the Monitor called as the twitching man groped his way doorward.

"Now maybe we can talk," Blondel suggested. "You said—"

"Only two of you left, out of seven." The Monitor shook his head sadly. "I had such high hopes—"

"I guess I'll go sit in one of my car bodies," the dull youth announced, rising abruptly.

"Sir—don't leave now, I beg of you! I can arrange for your potentiality testing, and synaptic acceleration therapy, at once! I guarantee you an increase in effective IQ of at least—"

The boy had blundered past him and was halfway to the steps. The Monitor hurried after him, pleading.

"Don't waste your time," Blondel called after him. "Tell me more about this subterranean factory idea, and—"

Halfway down the steps the Monitor overtook his quarry, jumped in front of him, and grasped his arm with both hands. "Sir, think what it could mean to you—"

The flimsy sleeve ripped free as the youth tugged against the restraint. The Monitor stumbled back, missed his footing, and fell. Blondel heard his head strike pavement with a sound like a dropped cantaloupe. The slender, gold-clad body curled on its side, making scratchy noises. Then it stiffened and was still.

"Oh-boy-oh-boy-oh-boy!" The youth circled the body. "Pa told me next time it was

the state farm fer sure." He fled at a sham-
bling run.

Blondel stopped, put a hand to the fallen
Monitor's chest. The pulse seemed strong,
but strangely rapid. And there was something odd about the feel of the chest. . . .

He grabbed the casualty under the arms,
laid him out face down in the shadow of a
flowering shrub. The uniform, he found, was
not secured by buttons. Instead, a pull at
just the right angle caused it to open down
the back. He turned the limp body over,
and tugged, peeling the jacket off over the
arms. It was stiff and bundlesome. It came
clear suddenly and Blondel was staring
blankly down at what was left lying on the
walk.

The face was still the same, and the neck;
but just below the collar line the texture
changed. The thorax was lumpy, pigeon-
chested, a shiny dark brown in color. And
the arms had come off with the blouse. All
that was left were a pair of limp, soft-looking
grayish flippers, like baby elephants trunks.

CHAPTER NINE

Blondel dropped the padded coat. It hit with a thump like wet laundry. For a second or two it seemed to him that his stomach was attempting to squeeze itself into a ball small enough to toss up with one heave. His next impulse was to run, but a form of shock-paralysis made his legs quiver like bass-viol strings. He took a shaky step back, and stumbled over the Monitor's gold-booted foot. At the jar, the Monitor's face tilted and fell off. Blondel saw a hollow shell like a Halloween mask dangling by a cluster of wires, exposing a head like a hairless seal, except that the eyes were below the mouth.

And, suddenly, it was all right. He was looking, not at a mutilated human but at an animal of a strange species. He let out a long breath, feeling his face muscles relax from the unconscious grimace in which they had been set.

He stood over the alien, listening. The campus-like park around him was still and peaceful. No other Monitors were in view along the curving walks. He licked his dry lips, pulled the unconscious alien farther back into the shadows, and set to work.

It was a difficult chore, stripping the remainder of the uniform from the fallen Monitor, because of the maze of wires, springs, and ducts that almost filled the pseudo-legs. The main power pack was built into the lower torso, with the organic body of the alien squatting on its dish-like upper surface. There was a snug little harness of woven metal around the thing, with leads running off in all directions, linking up what appeared to be servo-units built inside the knees and ankles. There was also a pair of electronic-looking devices, nestled where the armpits should have been, with connections to the mask. Some sort of sense boosters, Blondel decided. The mask itself was an intricate-looking piece of equipment, thick and heavy. The back was a porous gray material laced with color-coded filaments and bead-sized fittings, moulded to fit over the seal-head, but from the front it looked real enough to breathe. Every pore and eyelash was perfect; someone, Blondel reflected, had done a good job of costume design.

The uniform seemed to be a perfectly ordinary suit of clothes, once the muscle-shaped foam-rubber pads had been stripped from it. The hands had metal rod and spring cores, with padding, and outer gloves the color and texture of human skin lined on the inside with a fabric of metallic weave. They felt strange when he handled them, as though they were in business for themselves. Obeying the kind of impulse that makes a boy thrust a finger into an electric socket, Blondel tried one on. It snugged to his hand like a coat of paint. He flexed his fingers; the glove gave without strain. It was a perfect counterfeit.

He took the glove off and checked the remainder of the outfit. There were a number of apparati worked into the pads whose function was obscure. But a grain-of-rice hearing aid that tucked into his ear brought in the sound of moths flying fifty yards away; and a little device, fitted into a shirt button, kicked his hands away from the suit like an invisible rubber wall until he found the control in the heel of the left boot.

"A repellor field," Blondel muttered aloud. "No wonder nobody seems to be able to clobber a Monitor. And this is the outfit Blackwish wants to drop bombs on." He pocketed his finds and emerged from the concealment of the bushes. All around, the fairy lights twinkled across the peaceful gardens. He turned up his coat collar in a vague instinct for anonymity and set off at a brisk walk toward the nearest clump of trees.

From a semiconcealed position behind a Dempster-dumpster unit canted at the edge of a weed-grown vacant lot Blondel discerned the sagging contours of an independent cab parked at the curb, garish in purple and pink, blazoned with the mystic heraldry of fare formulae.

He took out Blackwish's bundled instructions, leafed past the countersigns and code data, found the alternate address for use in the event the Nixon Avenue headquarters had fallen to the foe: 72813 W. G. Harding Way, Room 213.

He checked the landscape again for hostile yellow figures, then nipped across through the tin cans and dead soldiers, leaned down beside the cab driver's window.

"You know where W. G. Harding Way is?" he hissed. The cabby sprang straight up, emitted a hoarse yell, and dived for the floor.

"Come up," Blondel urged. "This is no time to go to pieces. I need a cool driver who can get me across the city with important information."

The hackie showed Blondel a length of one-inch iron pipe. "The last wisey braced me from behind got twelve stitches," he stated truculently. "What are you, some kind of flatfoot?"

"Not exactly." Blondel opened the rear

door and got in. "Number 72813," he directed. "I'll lie on the floor. Don't waste any time."

The driver reared up and looked over the back of the seat.

"If you're tired, I'll take you to a hotel, Jack," he offered.

"I told you, I've got hot news to deliver! Let's get going!"

The driver shook his head sadly. "The town's gone nuts," he stated. "Ever since these Israelis taken over."

"What Israelis?"

"You know—the guys with the yellow suits."

"Oh, *those* Israelis—"

"Don't get me wrong," the cabby cautioned. "I'm Joosh myself. And you know the old saying—it takes one to know one."

"Security considerations prevent me from saying more," Blondel said. "But these Monitors are a lot more alien than—"

"I mean, in a way, you can't blame 'em. After two thousand years of being shoved around and with guys like Einstein on the team, it figures after a while they hadda make a move—you know what I mean?"

"Right," Blondel agreed. "If you see any Israelis, just wave and keep going. It wouldn't be convenient for me to be delayed right now."

"Hey!" The cabby eyed him sharply. "You ain't one of them anti-Semites?"

"Certainly not! It's just that this is private business—"

"You know, it's a funny thing, but some of my best friends are anti-Semitic," the cabby reflected. "Take O'Houlihan, my relief. For a lousy Mick, he ain't a bad guy—know what I mean?"

"Uh-huh. Look let's get moving—"

"Now, you take the Eyetalians. Catholics, just like the Irish, but with them we get along good."

"You *do* know where W. G. Harding Way is?"

"Now the Ayrabs—did you know the Arabs are Semites? But with them we don't get along good at all."

"There's no accounting for taste," Blondel pointed out.

"I know what you mean—you know what I mean?"

"Absolutely. Could we get started now?"

The cabby frowned down at him. "You with the CIA?"

"In a sense."

"Then you can count on me, pal. Like I says, I don't exactly blame them Israelis for getting a little fed up, but after all, this is the USA, right?"

"Right."

"And we don't need any bunch of foreigners telling us how to run the place, right?"

"Right. And if you'd—"

"Even if they are good Jewish boys."

"Exactly, so—"

"So let's get going, pal."

The cabby resumed normal driving position, clacked the flag down and pulled out into the empty street. The sound of the engine echoed off abandoned-looking storefronts.

"Them Israelis are making plenty changes," the cabby announced. "You know what they done? They give me another thirty-six hours in the hack game; then—phhht!"

"Don't keep slowing down," Blondel called.

"You want me to have a accident?" the driver inquired.

"Maybe later," Blondel muttered. "Can't you get a little more speed out of this hulk?"

"Nix, kid. I got a license to protect. By the way, what's this hot info you got?"

"Classified," Blondel said shortly.

"Oh. OK. I was in the Army, I know all about that kind of stuff."

"Good."

"I can keep my lip buttoned."

"Swell, so—"

"You can trust me."

"Great. Now if—"

"Like, if you was to tell me—"

"Not a chance."

"OK, OK, I ain't nosey! But like, if something was to happen to you—"

"No."

"Hah! Who needs it? The stuff *I* could tell *you*, pal!"

"Just drive," Blondel directed.

"For example, you know the mark-up on color television sets? I got a cousin—"

"I hate television," Blondel interrupted.

Several blocks passed in silence. Blondel, crouched awkwardly on the floor, raised his head and stole a glimpse from the window as the cab sped past a broad swathe of leveled ground where tall machines worked smoothly, erecting fragile-looking columns.

"Look at that," the cabby invited, staring at him in the rear-view mirror. "New synagogs going up all over town. Who says the Israelis got no engineering genius?"

"Not me," Blondel stated firmly. "Faster, please."

"Look, the way I see it, us American citizens got to stick together, right?"

"Right."

"So if you want to tell me—"

"Forget it."

The cabby sighed. "I got to hand it to you, Jack, you don't give away much. Here you are." He braked to a halt. Blondel peered out at the grim façades of empty stores under lightless walk-ups. One dim-lit entrance had the number 72813 lettered over it in peeling gilt. He stepped out.

"How much?"

"On the house," the hackie said. "My pleasure, pal. If I wasn't the father of nine, I'd side your play. Anyways, God Bless America." The hackie gunned away from the curb.

*   *   *

Blondel eyed the silent building front, looked both ways along the street. There was no one in sight. The cool evening air smelled of creosote and diesel fuel. He pushed through an imitation bronze door into a small vestibule containing a half-full rubbish can and a sway-backed bicycle. Narrow stairs upholstered in perished black rubber led upward. At the first landing, a massive gray door swung open with a lugubrious groan. In the hall, a dim light at the far end showed a rank of closed and silent doors. A faint light behind one threw a weak fan of yellow on the floor.

Blondel cocked his head, listening. There was no sound. He went along the corridor softly, paused at the lighted door. It bore the numerals 213 above letters that spelled out: *P. Gimlet. Importers.* He put an ear to the door, heard a sharp *bonk!* followed by a clink of glass and a gurgling sound.

Gently, Blondel tried the knob. Locked. He hesitated, then tapped lightly.

There was an interrogatory grunt from beyond the door, then footsteps. The latch rattled and the door swung wide. The angry face of General Blackwish stared out at him. "So there you are!" he barked.

"General! How did you get here? I thought—"

Maxwell's alert features appeared over the general's shoulder.

"Colonel," Blackwish snapped. "Arrest this man and prepare for a summary court martial!"

*   *   *

Roped to a wooden arm chair with a dozen turns of sash cord, Blondel looked around at the granite features of Blackwish, Maxwell, and two anonymous heavies with impact-thickened ears and fine scars on the cheekbones.

"I don't get it," he stated. "I spent the whole day scooting up and down back alleys and creeping through the underbrush looking for your loyal lieutenants so I could deliver your message, and when I find the place—you're there ahead of me, yelling treason!"

"Never underestimate a Blackwish," the general intoned.

"I thought Maxwell was plotting to kick you out and take over," Blondel reminded him.

"Don't attempt to sow dissension in the ranks." The general rocked back on his heels, showing his teeth. "We're a small band, perhaps, but our hearts are true."

"You said yourself—"

"Quiet, Blondel," Maxwell snapped. "You're only making it worse for yourself. Stealing an official copter was bad enough—"

"He gave it to me!"

"What did you do with the young woman you forced to accompany you?" Blackwish demanded. "Murder her and dump the violated body from the highjacked machine?"

"Nuts," Blondel said. "You know perfec—"
The room erupted in a striking display of

roman candles. Blondel admired them diz-
zily until they faded to reveal one of the
muscle-men standing before him, smiling
happily and rubbing his knuckles.

". . . tly well she went voluntarily," he
finished groggily.

"It's apparent to me that the man's an
arrant treacher," Blackwish said in a tone
of finality. "Entrusted with the sacred obligation to carry forward the good fight, he
defected to the borsht-and-vodka-swilling
enemy—"

"I didn't," Blondel said.

"Yes, you did," Blackwish contradicted
swiftly.

"I did not."

"You did, too."

"Did not!"

"You did, you did!"

"I didn't, I didn't."

"You did, you—"

"General," Maxwell interposed. "I think
the man's presence here, after you personally locked him in the cellar, is *prima facie*
evidence of his guilt. I think we'd better get
on with the distasteful business of carrying
out sentence—"

"Distasteful! Since when has the execution of traitors to the flag of this nation
been distasteful?"

"Well, as you know, sir, I'd love to do it,
but I've got this blister on my trigger finger
from addressing all those invitations to the
Victory Ball."

"That may have been a trifle premature, Colonel. We're not out of the woods yet."

"But you specifically ordered me to—"

"Don't quibble. Now about Blondel. Are we in agreement, then? I certainly don't want to seem arbitrary where a man's life is at stake."

"You're out of your minds!" Blondel protested. "All I did was—"

"As for disposal of the body," Blackwish said thoughtfully, "what would you think of drawing and quartering, as a warning to other would-be traitors?"

"General!" Blondel shouted. "I did my best to deliver your ridiculous message—"

"Too time-consuming," Maxwell judged. "I'd recommend a simple dismemberment, with the head impaled on a pole above the city gates."

"The city doesn't have any gates," Blondel interrupted. "And—"

"Fine idea, Colonel," Blackwish nodded. "I can see you're getting your old stuff back."

"Listen," Blondel appealed. "I've got some important information about the Monitors. They're—"

"Well, then, let's get it over with," Maxwell said. "I think perhaps Lance-Corporal Clinch here is the best man for the actual *coup de grâce*. Kenny, is your piece in order?" Maxwell looked inquiringly at one of the thugs.

"My what?" The man scowled.

"He means your gun, Kenny," Blackwish clarified.

"You didn't give me no bullets fer it," Kenny replied sullenly. "I ast you fer 'em plenty times, but no, you wouldn't—"

"Give Kenny some bullets, Colonel!" Blackwish snapped.

Maxwell checked his coat pockets, blew lint from the cartridges he found there, handed them across.

"You're not really going through with this?" Blondel inquired incredulously.

"My boy, you'll find, as you journey on through life, that the supreme penalty can be as easily administered by a small cadre of devoted patriots as by a giant totalitarian empire. Kenny, load your piece."

"My what?"

"He means your gun," Maxwell said.

"Listen to me!" Blondel tugged at the ropes. "I made a discovery this evening, about the Monitors! They're not human! I don't know what they are, but under those yellow uniforms—"

"Treated you as scurvily as you deserve, did they?" Blackwish curled his lip. "*Sic semper tyrannis!*"

"No—they treated me fine. As a matter of fact, I was right on the verge of starting to believe what they said. And then—"

"Note how coolly the swine confesses his guilt." Blackwish wagged his head "Boasts of it, even."

"He's a cool devil in the face of the firing

squad," Maxwell said grimly. "A pity he couldn't have been true blue."

"Look, I'm as true blue as the next guy! I'm trying to tell you, the Monitors are aliens! That's why—"

"Don't think to postpone your fate by a display of red herrings," Blackwish cautioned. "Of course the borsht-and-vodka-swilling invaders are aliens!"

"I mean *really* aliens! They have these little tentacles, and their heads are like upside-down seals, and—"

"Silence!" Blackwish shrilled. "The strain seems to have snapped your wits! The least you could do, as a former American, is to face your end like a man!"

"Of course," Maxwell put in over the exchange, "there *is* the alternative. . . ."

"I tell you, they're not human!" Blondel persisted. "They're intelligent aliens!"

"I'm not interested in the intellectual capacities of immigrants!" Blackwish countered. "Democracy will prevail no matter what weight of devilish ingenuity her enemies seek to employ against the defenders of the Republic!"

"About the alternative," Maxwell interjected.

"They're not just foreigners," Blondel insisted at the top of his voice. "They're inhuman! They came here from Mars—"

"A plea of insanity at this point will avail you nothing," Blackwish announced. "Kenny, do your duty!"

"The alternative." Maxwell tugged at the general's arm. "You're forgetting about the alternative!"

"There is no alternative to duty," Black-sh keened.

"Why don't you listen to me?" Blondel yelled.

"These bullets won't go in my piece," Kenny announced.

"Your what?" Blackwish roared.

"He means his gun," Blondel elucidated. "But if you shoot me—"

"We wanted to tell Blondel about the alternative." Maxwell was jumping up and down in front of the general. "The *alternative*, sir!"

"Americanism or nothing! That's the alternative!"

"I mean the alternative for Blondel!—instead of being shot!"

"What's that? You mean hanging?"

"General, I'm afraid in your zeal you've forgotten what we, er, I mean, there *is* another course open to Blondel, in case he decides to come to his senses!"

"What's that?" Blackwish looked suspicious.

"If he'll agree to fly the copter on the you-know-what mission, we won't have to carry out the sentence. Remember?" Maxwell said rapidly.

"Fly the copter?"

"You remember, General: When I discovered he was gone, and reminded you that we needed him to fly a certain very important mission, you agreed that we'd, ah, attempt to persuade him . . ."

"Hmmm . . . I seem to recall something of the sort. Escaped, didn't he? After I had personally locked him in the research lab?"

"Right, sir! And then you shrewdly guessed he might come here! Our ambush was successful, and now it's time to tell him about the alternative!"

"Very well. Tell him."

"Blondel," Maxwell faced him sternly, "there is one way in which you can avoid a traitor's death."

"If you're still thinking about your idiotic scheme to bomb their headquarters, forget it!" Blondel yelled. "If you'd just listen to what I'm trying to tell you—"

"OK if I just pound his brains out?" Lance-Corporal Clinch asked. "I can't get none of these here bullets in my gun."

"Piece," Blackwish corrected. "No, not just yet, Kenny."

"Nuts," Kenny said. "I never have no fun."

"We have at last," Maxwell said solemnly, "after seven-two hours of round-the-clock espionage activity by a number of intrepid SCRAG agents, discovered the location of the enemy headquarters."

"Yeah, I seen that on the telly," Kenny nodded. "Boy-oh-boy, some layout, huh, Blackwish?"

"*General* Blackwish to you, Lance Corporal!"

"As I said," Maxwell continued hastily, "we have pinpointed the target—"

"How come he gets to call me by my first name, and I got to call him General?" Kenny inquired loudly. "What kind of chicken—"

"That's enough, Kenny," Maxwell interrupted. "Having determined the co-ordinates of the Monitor HQ, it remains now for us to eliminate it. For this task we require a volunteer pilot."

"Where it's at," Kenny announced, "is out in the ocean, like. You ever heard of a place named Tortuga?"

"Kenny, why don't you go to the toilet while you have a chance?" Maxwell suggested.

"Gee, yeah." Kenny went away.

"Now, then." Maxwell rubbed his hands together briskly. "If you'd feel impelled to demonstrate your patriotism by offering your services for this glorious mission, I feel sure that the matter of your execution can be successfully deferred."

"At least until he gets back," Blackwish amended.

"Go rub salt in your nose," Blondel said loudly. "These Monitors aren't just a bunch of Russian commandos! I have proof that they're representatives of a superior culture from some planet out in space! Don't you realize what that means? If they have the technology for interstellar travel, they could squash anything we might throw at them like you'd step on a cockroach!"

"Oh-oh." Maxwell looked worried. "We went too far. He's cracked under the strain."

"He looks all right to me," Blackwish said. "I think the man's malingering!"

"If you start shooting, they'll take the wraps off and blow the planet right out of orbit!"

"Now, now, Blondel," Maxwell soothed, "don't be worried. We know just how to deal with little green men. We're just going to send a nice little bomb over that will blow them up before they can blow us up; you see?"

"I tell you, I know what I'm talking about! I'm not crazy! I saw one, with his disguise off! He was dark brown and shiny—"

"What did I tell you?" Blackwish crowed triumphantly. "Negroes in white-face, gentlemen! My worst fears realized! Inspired by the masters in the Kremlin, the Africans have at last emerged into the open!"

"They're not Africans! They're aliens! If you'd just look in my pocket—"

"Colonel," Blackwish said sternly, "I sense somehow that this man is not SCRAG timber. Keeps telling me the enemy is first one thing, and then another!"

"He's just upset, General," Maxwell said worriedly. "He'll be all right as soon as he sees that he has an alternative—"

Blackwish stepped back, crooked a finger at Maxwell. "You and I had better have a little talk," he said darkly. "I'm beginning to see the pattern here. The man's an obvious *agent provocateur,* sent in by the borsht-and-vodka-swilling enemy to confuse the clear issues of Americanism versus Red domination."

"But, General—"

"Just step out in the corridor with me for a moment, Colonel." Blackwish jerked his head at the silent heavyweight who had been standing by during the proceedings. "Oscar, place the Colonel under arrest until we've had time to go over his security record."

"But, General—"

"Outside." Blackwish stalked away, followed by Maxwell and silent Oscar.

Alone, Blondel tugged at the ropes binding his arms and legs to the chair. There seemed to be a little give in the loops thrown around his left wrist. He strained, wormed his hand free with no more than the loss of a little skin. Out in the hall, Blackwish's voice droned on, counterpointed by Maxwell's protestations.

The knots securing the right hand were almost out of reach. Blondel broke two fingernails before worrying the first strands free. Two minutes later he was massaging his numbed wrists. Then he bent to start in on the cords securing his ankles.

The side door clicked and swung open. Kenny entered, looking pleased. He held a 9mm Beretta in his right fist.

"I finally got a couple bullets in my gun,"

he announced. "Where do you want it, chum? Between the eyes OK?"

For a moment Blondel sat frozen, looking down the gaping barrel of the weapon in the Lance-Corporal's hand. He swallowed. His ears made a distinct popping noise, and the thought of the wonderful intricacy of the mechanism that was a human body flitted through his brain.

"Kenny," he heard himself saying carefully. "I think the general has changed his mind about shooting me. You see, he needs me to do a job—"

"Some guys is fussy about messing up the face," Kenny confided. He looked Blondel's features over critically. "But in your case, I guess it don't matter."

"Now, Kenny, the general's just stepped out. Why don't you just check with him—"

"Personal, I like the old beanshot because it's like quick, you know? A wrong slug in the gut, maybe a guy can kick around a while before he croaks." Lenny shook his head. "Sloppy, very sloppy."

"You see, we're all friends again, Kenny." Blondel managed a sickly grin. "He just forgot to have me untied—"

"So you can take your choice. Personal, I'd go for the knob, but you might be one of them guys likes a nice open-box funeral."

"Kenny, the general will be very upset if you shoot me now, because—"

"Don't yell," Kenny warned. "Now, snap

it up before the old coot comes back and louses up the whole caper." He lowered his voice. "The way he changes his mind all the time, I got a idea his marbles is loose, you know?"

"Yes, Kenny, you're right. Now, I have a proposal for you. How would you like to see something very unusual?"

Kenny nodded. "OK. But look, I got a job to do—"

"It's something I want you to have. I'd hate to think of the general getting it. Now don't shoot me before I can show you."

Kenny frowned. "You got dough on you?" He shifted the gun to his left hand.

"Not exactly money; something much better. Just let me get it out of my pocket—"

"Watch it!"

"No guns, Kenny. Just a little souvenir I picked up. . . ." He groped in his pocket, brought out the grain-of-rice hearing aid he had taken from the fallen Monitor.

"Now, Kenny." Blondel licked dry lips. "This little device will enable you to hear flies walking on the ceiling."

"So?" Kenny raised his shoulders. "Who wants to hear flies walking?"

"How about this?" Blondel tried again, found the button-sized repellor-field generator. "You just twiddle this, and nobody can get near you."

"Yeah, I seen stink-bombs before. That ain't worth no big dough."

Blondel was frantically rummaging for

the control unit from the Monitor's boot-heel, instead encountered the gloves.

"What's that?" Kenny leaned forward.

"These are, ah, gloves." Sparring for time, Blondel pulled one on. "Nice, don't you think?" He displayed the gloved hand. "Just the thing for special occasions—"

"Nuts," Kenny said. "I think you're stalling, Bo—"

"Now, Kenny . . ." Blondel gripped the arms of the chair. "Don't do anything hasty . . ." His hands closed, tensing for the impact as Kenny raised the pistol. "If you'll just wait a couple of seconds, we'll both avoid a big mistake. . . ."

"Hey!" Kenny was frowning darkly at Blondel's right hand. "What you doing to the chair?"

Blondel looked down, only then noticing a curious sensation in his right hand. The left, ungloved hand was gripping the polished hardness of oak; but under the right hand, snugged into the Monitor's glove, the wood had collapsed like damp *papier-mâché*.

"What's the idea busting up the furniture?" Kenny demanded.

Blondel opened his hand. The glove seemed a trifle warm to the touch, but otherwise was as light and supple as a silk driving glove. He poked at the wood. It felt as hard as wood usually felt. He cautiously squeezed the chair arm again. There was a soft crunching sound, as the tough material yielded into splinters. It felt, Blondel decided, like undercooked spaghetti.

"Geeze!" Kenny gaped at the spectacle.

Blondel gripped the edge of the wooden seat and squeezed. The wood went flat, with a sound like walnut shells underfoot. Kenny stepped closer, his mouth open, his eyes fixed on the enchanted hand. Blondel reached, gripped the muzzle of the gun between thumb and forefinger, and pinched it flat. Kenny hardly noticed. He watched dumbly as Blondel nipped off the ropes on his legs and stood.

"Just go stand in the corner, now, Kenny," Blondel directed. "When the general comes back, tell him I had to hurry along to a magician's convention. He needn't bother to chase me, because I'll be using my cloak of invisibility and my flying carpet. Be good, now." He edged around the paralyzed Lance Corporal and exited through the side door.

CHAPTER TEN

Blondel sought out the back stairs, descended silently, emerged in a rubbish-packed back alley. He followed it until it debouched into a cramped rectangle of lumpy black-top under a towering billboard announcing the availability of Jewels on Credit. Something dark and massive loomed in the deep shadows against a lichenous wall of kidney-colored brick. It was the SCRAG Z-car.

Blondel started past it, then paused.

Dashing to SCRAG headquarters with the news of the true nature of the Invader had been a serious error in judgment. But if he could get through to Washington now, it might not be too late. There, if anywhere, some still-organized remnant of U. S. sovereignty might yet be found. And with the information he could supply—plus the miracle gadgets in his pockets . . .

The rest was a little vague, but the immediate objective was obvious. The car was waiting. True, it was a trifle conspicuous. But if he could reach open country it might well slip through, what with its armor, radar-negative gear, and cross-country speed. So far, every move he had made to join the resistance to the invaders had ended in a hung jury. Now, at last, direct action was at hand. He took a moment to lift the access panel over the rear-mounted power plant and check for TNT charges, found none.

As he reached for the door there was a stir behind him. Something icy cold touched the back of his neck.

"Yeah," a thin voice mumured near his right ear. "It's a gat. You the guy who owns this crate?"

"Ahhherrrummm! . . . Yes," Blondel decided quickly. "But you can have it. I don't need it anymore. It's a terrible gas-eater, and as for parking the thing—"

"Good," the voice cut him off. "Nasty Jack wants to see you."

"Ah. . . . Nasty Jack?"

"Let's go. We'll take my car."

"Look, there's something I'd like to confess—"

"Save it for Sunday." The gat poked a little harder. "Shake it, rube."

"About the Z-car—"

There was a soft click as the safety went off the gun. Blondel moved hastily off in the indicated direction, fetched up beside the dark-gleaming, chrome-fitted bulk of a late-model hearse.

"Inside. If you handle yourself nice, you get to finish the trip sitting up."

"Can't we talk this over? You're making a serious mistake—"

"Some guys got wrong ideas about when to flap their lip," the voice grated. "Inside! Drive slow and stick to the back streets. If they spot us, go into high and we'll find out if the guy was lying about what this can will do."

Silently, Blondel slid behind the wheel, started up, maneuvered the heavy car out into the dark street.

Forty minutes of cautious travel by circuitous routes which skirted the growing islands of Monitorial reconstruction brought them to a section of blocky, porticoed houses perched at the edges of truncated lawns fronting cracked sidewalks.

"Next left." The command came from the darkness. Blondel complied.

"Turn in here." Blondel swung into a graveled drive, pulled to a stop beside a stately old frame house shaded by lofty elms, its façade gleaming a ghoulish pale blue in the glow from a large rectangular sign planted in the center of the lawn, discreetly announcing "Personalized Care For Your Loved Ones."

"Get out."

"Uh, there's something I really think I ought to explain before this goes any further," Blondel started.

"Tell Jack. He likes to listen to guys try to explain."

They crossed the lawn, rounded the house to a side door; Blondel's guide rapped three times, then two, then four. Nothing happened.

"Hey, Max!" he shouted.

"Yeah?" The door opened and an unshaven man with a fat, pale face looked out. Blondel responded to a poke in the lumbar vertebrae, stepped into a spacious kitchen redolent of tomato paste and Chianti.

"This is the mug Jack was wanting to talk to."

The fat man frisked Blondel in a bored way, nodded.

"Go on in."

Again the prod from behind. Blondel twitched, thinking of the glove in his coat pocket, the repellor-field gear—

"Don't stall, rube." At an extra-sharp jab he fairly leaped through a swing door and was in a room of corroded rococco elegance, staring at a man who sat alone at the head of a long table, peeling a grape with a penknife.

"Meet Nasty Jack," the voice behind him

said. "Don't do nothing, don't say nothing, unless he tells you to."

The man called Nasty Jack was lean, dark, with shiny Valentino hair and a gold tooth. The sleeves of his purple silk shirt were held up by diamond-studded arm-bands, and another diamond, the size of an elk's tooth, impaled his yellow knit tie. He thrust the grape into his mouth, chewed thoughtfully, looking Blondel over, spat the seeds on the tablecloth.

"So you're a general, hah?" His voice was a bass rumble.

"No, I'm not, and if that nitwit who brought me here would have listened to me—"

"Got busted, hey?" Nasty Jack nodded understandingly. "The same thing happened to me, the time I was in the army. Some stoolie from the IG claimed I was renting out recruits at a buck fifty an hour to crooked contractors. Three stripes and a rocker down the drain." Jack poured dusky red wine from a bottle, into a jelly glass, swallowed it whole.

"You don't seem to get the idea—" Blondel started.

"But I'm broad-minded, General," Jack cut him off. "As far as I'm concerned, once a general, always a general."

He folded the knife with a flick of the thumb and dropped it into the pocket of a checkered vest. "Now let's talk over this deal of yours."

"If you'd let me explain—"

Jack waved away the offer. "Everybody falls off the wagon once in a while, General," he said. "The only difference, you and me got caught." He leaned forward. "You still ready to go ahead with the proposition?"

"As a matter of fact—"

"Because in case you had a change of plans, General, Nasty Jack is not the guy to take it calm. Get me?"

"Certainly. But—"

"So that just leaves the details to iron out, right?"

"Well . . ."

"OK." Jack poked a finger at Blondel. "Now, how soon can you have the dough ready?"

"The dough . . . ?"

"I hope you got no funny ideas about the dough, General," Jack said ominously.

"No, no, of course not. It's just that—well, we generals have a lot on our minds. I seem to have sort of forgotten some of the details."

"Geez!" Jack looked at him admiringly. "Any guy which can forget a detail like five million iron men in gold is the kind of operator to which I take my hat off to!"

"Sure," Blondel swallowed. "Five million. How thoughtless of me—"

"So—just as soon as you make delivery, the skilled manpower of my organization is ready to go, just like I told you." Jack leaned

back and smiled. His gold tooth threw back
a sinister reflection from the candle-shaped
bulb in the unshaded socket on the wall.

"Your, ah, organization," Blondel stalled.
"Ummm, skilled manpower . . ."

"Now, I'm not the nosey type, General,"
Jack raised his hands, fending off the idea.
"I don't know exactly what you got in mind.
But Central Headquarters for American National Crime, Robbery, and Extortion is
strictly a patriotic group. We're with you
all the way—as soon as I get the dough."

"Behind me," Blondel gulped.

"As Chairman of CHANCRE, let me tell
you, General, you're getting a loyal bunch
of boys, ready to do their bit for freedom."

"Freedom." Blondel nodded. "Well, that
certainly sounds . . ." He paused. "You say
they're . . . ready to do their bit . . . ?"

"Damn right! General, if there's one thing
the membership of CHANCRE is against,
it's better law-enforcement. And from what
I seen of these Monitors, once they're in the
saddle, the good old days are on the way
out fast!"

"How many men have you got?" Blondel
inquired crisply.

"About six thousand skilled technicians,
all equipped with bullet-proof vests, two-
way wrist radios, and records as long as
your arm, each and every one. In a word,
reliable pros; none of these punk red-hots
which they seen a little television and think
they're Al Capone."

"Jack," Blondel leaned forward tensely, "those other plans—they're out the window. Something new has come up."

Jack scowled. "Just a minute, General! A doublecross—"

"Skip the commercial," Blondel cut in. "This is important. We both want the same thing: to get rid of the Monitors. Now pass that wine bottle over here and let's get down to some serious discussion. There are a couple of things you ought to know about . . ."

"Martians, hey?" Jack shook his head self-critically. "I should of figured that one myself. I knew there was something creepy about that mob. They're all over this town like grated cheese on a plate of *pasta*, but they steer clear of my little place of business here like it was poison. I check with a couple colleagues, and they tell me the same thing: not one customer in a yellow suit. Believe me, General, with as many of these dudes as we got in town, that ain't natural."

"Now, my idea is that everyone in the country will feel the same way you and I do, Jack," Blondel pursued his point. "All we have to do is get the information to the public. The minute they realize we've been invaded by nonhuman monsters from outer space, they'll spontaneously rise in a body."

"With the odds a couple hundred million of us patriotic citizens to maybe a hundred thousand of them, how can we lose?" The

CHANCRE chief looked at his solid gold strap watch.

"If I get on the hook right now, I can catch Vito in Brooklyn, Ricco in Detroit, Carlo in Washington, Dino in Philly, Sacco in Albany, Ralph in Pittsburgh—"

"Ralph?"

"I see you got the same old idea that all hoods are Italians," Jack said pityingly. "I'm calling a general meeting of the whole Board of Directors for ten o'clock tonight. By that time, General, you better have everything set. We got no time to waste if we're going to put the country back in the hands of the common people."

From his chair at the head of the long table, Nasty Jack waved a gold-tipped cigarette toward Blondel and said: "Take it, General. The boys are listening."

Blondel looked along the row of expectant faces. With the exception of one or two eye-patches and crumpled ears, they looked like nothing so much as a group of respectable county commissioners, meeting to divide up the week's haul of bribes.

He cleared his throat. "Gentlemen," he announced, "our only hope of success depends on split-second timing and perfect co-ordination. Our first move will be to seize the radio and TV stations in selected cities, and put the news on the air. At the same time, we distribute leaflets, hitting every major city between Boston and Miami.

Simultaneously, our runners cover the same areas on foot and bicycle, passing out proclamations."

"Nice," Jack nodded. "I can see how you made your star, General. Now, on the print contracts, I got a cousin—"

"No nepotism, Jack," Blondel said sternly. "This is for the good of the country. Remember?"

"What's good for private enterprise, is good for the country," Jack retorted. "That's what Abraham Lincoln, or one of them guys, said."

"I think you're quoting him out of context," Blondel rebutted.

"Chief, you want I should rub out this monkey?" a scholarly-looking member inquired from his place.

"Keep your dukes away from your rod, Angelo," Jack said sternly. "You ain't got the eye for a precision assignment. Besides, when I want the general plugged, I'll say so."

"Maybe we'd better get on with the plans," Blondel said hastily. "I've drawn up a list of clear-channel stations that can blanket the eastern seaboard. I don't know exactly what techniques the Monitors are using to jam our broadcasts, but I'm pretty sure that possession of these transmitters is the key to the situation." He handed out sheets of paper which were passed from hand to hand along the table.

"You boys know the situation in your own

areas," Jack stated. "So how about it? Let's have some proposals from the floor on the best way to knock 'em off without busting 'em up."

"I got a better idea," a member offered. "Let's pass this jazz, and knock off a couple banks instead. I know of a couple over Duluth way which they're practically begging for it."

"Yeah," another chimed in. "We can fix up soldier-boy here with a cement overcoat and let him go for a swim in the lake—"

"Nuts," contributed a third. "Why mess with banks, when the mint is sitting right there in DC—and nobody watching it but some nancies in yellow pants?"

Jack dipped into the coat pocket and produced a large, business-like automatic. He rapped on the table with it and cleared his throat menacingly.

"Objections overruled," he announced. "General, go ahead with the plan."

"Ah—the leaflets will have to be ready twenty-four hours before M-minute," Blondel went on. "The bicycle corps will have to move out as soon as possible thereafter, and be in position—"

"Nobody ain't going to get me on no bicycle," a stout, bishop-like member stated flatly. Jack fingered the gun and looked at him thoughtfully.

". . . Unless I feel like riding a bicycle," the man added. Jack lifted the gun and weighed it on his hand.

". . . And it just so happens I feel like it," the speaker concluded, looking around defiantly. "And when I feel like riding a bicycle, there ain't nobody that can stop me from riding a bicycle."

"You ain't riding no bicycle, Mario," Jack told him.

". . . Unless I change my mind."

"And . . . ?"

"And I just changed my mind," Angelo muttered, subsiding.

"Now, our best bet for taking the stations is to infiltrate them in advance," Blondel said into the conversational gap. "We'll need forty picked crews of about twenty men, dressed up as fans and equipped with autograph books and guitars."

"What's with the guitars?" a tiny, spider-like member with a prominent Adam's apple demanded. "We got fast cars, and plenty of ammo. I say we fan out and plug every yellow-back we see, and any incidental coppers that maybe are still running around loose. Then we move on to DC and clean *it* out. Then we round up all the congressmen we can find, shoot 'em, and appoint ourselves to fill out the terms."

"Fiorella, you are a dirty, lousy, un-American rat," Jack cut him off coldly. "Boys—take him for a ride in the country."

"Hey—wait a minute!" Fiorella protested, as his neighbors rose and closed in. "So OK, I was out of line—" Large hands clamped

on him, lifted him bodily, bore him doorward, kicking futilely.

"Don't take the Caddie," Jack called. "I
just had it washed. Now"—he looked around
at the others—"where were we?"

"Just infiltrating the radio stations,"
Blondel said. "Remember, violence is no
good; but it—"

There was a sharp *rat-tat-tat-tat!* from
outside. Nasty Jack looked up with an an-
noyed expression. "I told them punks to
take a run out in the boondocks," he said.
"But no, they got to litter up the back yard."

"As I was saying, violence is out," Blondel
pressed on. "The Monitors have equipment
that will protect them from anything we
can throw at them. We'll have to use trick-
ery and passive resistance—"

"Hey, Jack," Mario spoke up. "How does
this pigeon get the inside info on the yellow-
backs? What is he, some kind of stoolie?"

"Yeah, no gats, he says," Angelo joined
in. "This pansy is a like plant, if youse ask
me—"

"I'm a no lika thees beez," a blue-jowled
fellow growled. "Whatsa good we gotta machines gun, we no usa, hah?"

"Quiet, Ralph." Jack raised a hand. "The
General here scouted around and done some
nifty inside work. He knows what he's talking about."

"Sez he," someone growled.

"I'll show you a sample of their work."

Blondel took out the glove and slipped it on, just as a rap sounded at the door.

"Yeah?" Nasty Jack bellowed.

"There's a guy out here, he wants you should talk to him," a muffled voice sounded through the panel.

"Tell him to drop dead, I'm busy!"

"Boss, I think maybe you ought to talk to the bum."

"OK . . . OK. Send him in."

"He wants you should come out."

Jack slapped the table with both hands. "Boy! What I got to put up with." He rose, went to the door. As he opened it, a thunderous *bam-bam-bam-bam!* roared, racketing between the walls, sending dust flying from sudden craters in the opposite wall. Blondel whirled in time to see Jack fly backward into the room, slam the floor on his back, and slide. The tiny figure of Fiorella came through the door, dwarfed by the Thompson submachine gun in his hands.

"No artillery, hah?" he inquired brightly of the assembled spectators. "I told you his clutch was slipping." He handed the gun to a subordinate, drew a yellow hankie from the breastpocket of his fawn-colored suit, dabbed at his forehead, and took the chair vacated by the former CHANCRE chief.

"OK." He rubbed his hands together and gave Blondel a piercing look. "Now let's decide what to do about this wisey and his big ideas, eh, boys?"

*   *   *

"If you idiots would listen to me," Blondel appealed for the fourteenth time, "you'd realize that none of your schemes for butchering Monitors is going to work! Our only chance is to arouse the populace by exposing them as invaders from space—"

"You slobs are all wrong," Ricco stated. "We ought to dump this mug in the lake tonight, or maybe first thing in the morning on account of it's too late to get a couple yards of ready-mix delivered today."

"Yeah, all we ever get to do is plug guys," Vito mourned. "I read in the comics all these swell capers, how they string guys up by the thumbs, and strap 'em down to the streetcar tracks, and dump 'em in melted iron, and all. But us, we got to go the conservative route: *bing! bing!* and it's all over."

"You got to sacrifice some of the glamor for high production," Fiorella pointed out patiently. "Also, we got the public relations angle to figure. You throw a guy off the Trib tower, and some pedestrian is liable to get hurt. You got to be safety conscious."

"So, OK, we tie his wrists to the back bumper of a car, and his feet to the front piazza, and—"

"Why don't you listen?" Blondel demanded. "Time is growing short—"

There was a rap at the door. "Hey, Fiorella," someone called. "There's a guy out here wants to see you."

The little man drew a large watch from his vest pocket and studied it.

"Twenty minutes," he wagged his head sadly. "It don't take long for the rot to set in."

"He says it's important," the voice persisted.

"Carlo, you go," Fiorella directed hopefully. Carlo shook his head silently.

"Look, you guys ain't even give me a chance I should explain my program," the recently-appointed leader protested.

"Better go ahead, Boss," Rocco said in an ominous tone.

"Yeah, if there's one thing us boys don't stand for, it's a chief which he's got a yellow streak," Sacco said.

Fiorella pushed back his chair. "Sometime I wonder why I bucked so hard for the job."

"Remember Jack," Ricco encouraged. "He looked pretty good going out that door."

"Yeah, but he didn't look so hot coming back in." Fiorella squared his narrow shoulders, marched to the door, threw it wide with a dramatic gesture and braced himself. However, no shots rang out.

"He's in the living room, boss," Max's voice was audible. "He says . . ." The conversation was cut off by the closing door.

"Now, fellows," Blondel said into the heavy silence in the room. "Let's forget past differences and face up to the fact that the freedom and independence of humanity are at stake here. We've got to stop all this bickering and take effective action before everybody in the country has joined Happy Horinip's Quota Toppers and settled down to the role of subject race—"

"Now's the time, boys," Ricco said flatly. "While nobody ain't looking." He flicked his wrist and a snub-nosed Walther .635 appeared from nowhere, nestled in his palm.

"Fiorella won't like it if he comes back and finds another mess on the rug," Vito predicted.

"I'll just croak him barehanded," Carlo offered, rising.

Blondel got to his feet and backed away from the table. "Fellows, you're making a great mistake! The Monitors are the enemy, not little old me!"

Ricco stood, planted himself solidly, placed his left hand on his left hip, raised the gun and brought it down carefully, drawing a bead.

"Right through the gravy stain under the first button," he called the shot. "No fair moving, now, Buster."

Blondel squeezed his eyes shut. "Don't do it—" His words were drowned by the shattering report of a gun. He waited for a moment for the pain to hit, then opened one eye in time to see Ricco drop his gun and tumble to the rug. Fiorella stood in the doorway, blowing smoke from the business end of a large revolver.

"I turn my back five minutes, and you mugs start clowning," he said in an aggrieved tone. "Don't nobody shoot the Rube.

It looks like maybe we got a use for him, after all."

"Thanks very much, Fiorella," Blondel started, feeling his legs begin to wobble in reaction to the excitement of the last few moments. "You'll never regret—" He broke off as the CHANCRE chief stepped back and waved a dark-cloaked figure into the room.

"It looks like poor old Jack, are eye pee, missed a couple bets," Fiorella said. "Boys"—he indicated the newcomer—"meet the real General Blackwish."

"A heart attack, you say?" The general eyed the sprawled corpse of Nasty Jack with distaste. "In that case, what accounts for the holes in his chest?"

"Moths," Fiorella said succinctly. "Now, General, since you tipped us off this monkey is a ringer, which we was going to do away with him anyway, I don't exactly get the reason why you was in such a sweat to keep him alive. Ricco was one of my best boys, and—"

"Men," Blackwish looked sternly along the table. "We face an enemy of awesome power. Traditional offensive techniques are useless against them. In that, Blondel was right." He paused, impressively. "But we at SCRAG have the answer."

"What's the question?" Vito asked, puzzled.

"The question is survival!" Blackwish's fist struck the table a resounding blow. "To harass them with mere guns is futile! To attempt lesser measures, such as the visionary scheme to discredit them with wild stories of extraterrestrial origin is nonsense! Only one course is open to us: Instant, total, utter annihilation of their headquarters in a single, irresistible blow!"

"You can't—" Blondel started.

"Gentlemen," Blackwish purred, "we have located this target. It consists of an immense floating fortress—a manmade island over five miles in length—anchored in the south Atlantic, some thirty miles south southeast of Dry Tortuga."

"They have defensive screens that will stop anything you can drop on them!" Blondel interrupted. "If you'd give me a chance, I could show you—"

"Our weapon," Blackwish's voice rose, "is of such a nature that no defense can stand against it!"

"You'll never get it to the target," Blondel persisted. "They have a repellor field—"

"Have you gentlemen ever heard," Blackwish shouted him down, "of an implosion bomb?"

"How's about if we hit the First National," Carlo proposed. "It ain't a fancy bank, but it's solid, you know? My old man knocked it off once, back in '28, and he says to me, Carlito—"

"I don't care what kind of weapon you've got," Blondel yelled. "A stack of H-bombs won't do any good if you can't get them through—"

"H-bombs?" Blackwish smiled grimly. "Child's toys," he dismissed them. "The implosion bomb is based on a new principle: A core of annihilated matter into which the surrounding material is forced by pressures comparable to those at the heart of a star! The result: A localized collapse of the very fabric of space. In short—implosion on a titanic scale!"

"How you figure to get this bomb out to this here island?" Sacco demanded.

"I have a miniature SCRAG copter of advanced design," Blackwish said. "At this moment it is concealed under a tarpaulin behind the greenhouse, where my men placed it earlier this evening. The bomb is aboard, armed and ready."

"What's to keep 'em from shooting it down?" Carlo queried.

"Experience has shown that the Monitors are incapable of intercepting our aircraft," Blackwish replied.

"Nuts," Blondel commented. "I think they let aircraft through because they don't want to injure anybody by forcing them to crash-land."

"Who's supposed to fly this baby out there?" Mario inquired.

"That, gentlemen, is where Mr. Blondel enters the picture," Blackwish stated. "He happens to be an experienced pilot."

"I won't do it," Blondel said loudly. "It

would be asking for reprisals on the whole human population!"

"Is that the only reason you need the mug?" Fiorella raised his eyebrows.

"The reason seems to me to be sufficient!" Blackwish snapped. "It happens that SCRAG has no qualified aeronautical specialists in its ranks."

"Yeah?" Fiorella snapped his cigarette butt over his shoulder and picked up his revolver. He spun the cylinder, then turned to face Blondel.

"I used to be Navy," he said. "I got over four thousand hours in jets. I'll take your bomb in, General. And we can dump this mug right now, which I don't trust him no farther than I can throw him."

"Oh-oh, here we go again." Blondel watched the gun muzzle swing to bear on him. "Look, give me thirty seconds, OK? Just to show you what I'm talking about. . . ." He fumbled desperately in his pockets, turned up a stick of Wrigley's, several pennies, the miniature hearing aid—and the tiny control device taken from the Monitor's boot-heel.

"That is it." He held it up. "You just turn this little know knob here—"

The *blam!* of the .44 revolver filled the room with acrid smoke. Blondel felt a light tap at his chest, followed instantly by a sensation of heat that swept over him and faded at once. Fiorella lowered the gun, peering through the smoke.

"Hey." Someone waved his hands to clear away the obscuring veil. "He's still sitting up!"

"Kind of short range for a miss, chief," Sacco commented. "But don't worry . . ." He brought his gun up and fired. Again Blondel felt the light blow, this time directly over the heart. Sacco's confident grin faded as he blinked at Blondel, still sitting rigid in the chair. The gunman turned the weapon so as to look down the barrel.

"It ain't never done that before," he said. "All I done was pull the trigger—" There was a deafening bang and Sacco executed a back-flip, flopped around for a few seconds, and lay still. There seemed to be considerable blood.

Fiorella, holding the big revolver in both hands now, with the butt resting on the table, held it out at arm's length, the muzzle almost touching Blondel's shirt front. Blondel, still sitting as if paralyzed, roused himself suddenly, reached, caught the gun in his hand.

"This is what I was trying to tell you," he said. "It's the repellor field—"

"My . . . my gun," Fiorella quavered, staring at it. The barrel was folded almost double. Fiorella carefully placed the weapon on the table before him. It looked like squeezed modeling clay.

"Here, what's this?" Blackwish queried. "What . . . what . . . ?"

Vito's gun whipped up, fired twice. Blondel reached out, put his palm over the smoking muzzle just as the third round fired. The resultant explosion sent four members of the CHANCRE steering committee sprawling, bleeding from multiple contusions, and knocked Vito over backwards, to sit up cursing, holding his shattered hand. Blondel jumped up, knocking his chair over, backed around the table.

"Grab him!" a survivor yelled weakly. Hands reached cautiously—and were thrown back by what seemed to be an invisible barrier six inches from Blondel's body. Blackwish recoiled in his chair, his mouth open. The CHANCRE men still functioning backed away, hands raised.

"You're all a bunch of idiots," Blondel said. "Maybe between us we could have accomplished something, but all I've gotten have been double-crosses, excuses, and assassination attempts. OK. I'm through trying to line up any help. I'll do it alone. Just stay where you are. I'm leaving now." They watched dumbly, as Blondel stepped over the various bodies on the floor and opened the door.

The dumpy figure of Max stood in the hall, the Thompson gun aimed across his hip. It jumped, spouting red fire, and Blondel felt the rapid *slap-slap* as the heavy slugs struck the shield around him. He kept coming, and Max tossed the Thompson into the air and dived for cover.

No one else barred his way. He went along the drive, past the black gleam of the hearse, crossed a formal lily garden, saw the shrouded shape projecting from the bushes beside a small greenhouse. He pulled it out, stripped off the tarp. The contraption thus exposed resembled a cross between a vacuum cleaner and a diving suit.

A hoarse call came from behind him; he turned.

"Blondel . . . !" It was General Blackwish, coming across the lawn, waving an arm excitedly. "It's my duty to inform you that I've declared martial law here!" he hooted. "In the name of the Federal Government I'm ordering you to place yourself at the disposal of the nearest military commander, who happens to be myself! I'm also commandeering for official use the bulletproof vest you're wearing, as well as any other items of military value you may have in your possession!"

"Go soak your eyeballs," Blondel retorted. "I'm taking your flying pogo stick, General. I hope it's got plenty of fuel aboard."

"That's government property!" Blackwish protested, as Blondel deployed the folding blades, unbuckled the straps which secured the pilot to the saddle. "I'm warning you this is an act of open treason!"

"Where's the bomb stowed?" Blondel demanded.

"My lips are sealed," Blackwish declared, backing away.

"General, I don't have any time to waste. It's a long way to Dry Tortuga."

"You wouldn't deliver your nation's secret weapon to the enemy?" Blackwish's face looked purple in the moonlight.

"Isn't that what you wanted?"

"I . . . you mean . . . am I to understand you'll fly the SCRAG mission?"

"I guess that's up to me, eh, General?"

Blackwish's face twitched with strain. "I . . . I suppose I have no choice but to place the destiny of America in your hands," he managed. "Surely you—a former commissioned officer of the American armed forces—will not betray that high trust?"

"The bomb."

"There." Blackwish indicated a pouch attached to the main supporting column of the tiny machine. Blondel opened it, lifted out a heavy cylindrical object no larger than a salt shaker.

"Is this all there is to it?"

"It's armed and ready," Blackwish said in a hushed tone. "It's necessary merely to give it a brisk rap. Dropping it from waist height onto a hard floor will do nicely."

Blondel tucked the bomb gingerly into his pocket, then inserted himself into the loose-fitting coverall that served as pilot's compartment, settled himself in the saddle. The straps buckled securely across his knees, tying him in place. He tilted the plastic helmet down over his head, snugged his feet to the control pedals.

"You *will* drop it, won't you, Blondel?" Blackwish's voice was faint through the headpiece. "You won't yield to any insane impulse to defect to the borsht-and-vodka-swilling enemies of the democratic way of life?"

"It's about a three-hour flight," Blondel said. "Maybe by the time I get there I'll have the answer to that one."

He studied the controls, flipped a switch, depressed a key. The rotors came to instant life. He grabbed the steering levers, angled the abruptly lifting machine away from the outspread branches of a tree. He looked back, caught one glimpse of the foreshortened figure staring up after him. Then darkness closed in, and he was alone, rising fast into the inky night sky.

CHAPTER ELEVEN

Riding the pocket copter, Blondel decided after the first ten minutes, was the closest approach to a witch's broomstick that had yet been devised. Still, it was not as uncomfortable as it looked. The saddle was nicely padded, the coverall windproof, fleece-lined, and electrically heated; the bubble helmet light and transparent, pressurized with oxygen-enriched air. At ten thousand feet he leveled off, studied the instrument faces set in the handlebar of the machine, set off on a heading of one-oh-five at an airspeed of one hundred and ten MPH. The engine hummed smoothly; the slip stream howled around the cleverly designed full-length windshield which deflected the worst of the air blast. Above, the short blades whined, chopping at the air at ten thousand RPM, hurtling him onward.

Below, through scattered cloud cover, he saw the city slipping away to the west—a vast sprawl of misty light interrupted in great, rectilinear patches by the Monitor-made clearings. Almost half the city, he estimated, had now been leveled by the invaders.

The first hour passed. Blondel shifted against the holddown straps, conscious of the weight of the implosion bomb nestled in his pants pocket. Blackwish's scheme had been insane, of course—but his own was probably no better. The Monitors, pacifistic though they were, undoubtedly had effective methods of preventing airborne attackers—even gnat-sized attackers like himself—from getting too close. But since all other approaches had failed, there was only this one forlorn hope left. One man, one tiny infernal device, which might or might not perform as advertised, and another thousand miles of empty air to traverse before he would know the answer.

Dawn came after an endless night: a glory of dusky pink swelling to gold and then to a flat, wintry blue. Blondel squinted out across the olive-drab blanket below, cut by the silver threads of rivers, patched by tilled acreage, blotched here and there by towns and cities, and crisscrossed by roads that wandered along routes originally marked out by beavers or elk or settlers pursuing lost goats. Far off to the north the mighty coast-to-coast highway, designed by the Monitors, was a rigid line of pale pink—a strange color for paving, Blondel thought. But then, why not?

The day wore on. Once a gold-painted heli flitted under him on a skew course, a bright dragonfly in the sunlight; but it made no move to intercept him. He climbed then, leveled at fifteen thousand. Far ahead, the metallic sheen of the sea stretched to the horizon. Blondel remembered the last meal he had eaten—lunch with Nelda at the empty restaurant with the insidious Pekkerup hovering like an officious mother hen. It seemed too long ago, like a game of mud patties in another life.

And then the coast was under him, a long curve of slate-blue, steely ocean stretching from the line of slow-combing breakers edging the beach on and on to the distant haze of the horizon.

It was mid-afternoon before he discovered the chocolate bars, dates, and water supply tucked neatly away in a pouch just below the left knee of the coverall. He ate slowly, savoring every bite, using only a few sips of water. If the Monitors' floating island was not in the advertised position, it might be a long trip across the ocean. . . .

The first tentative yellowing of evening was touching the farthest clouds when Blondel sighted the incredible shape lying on the sea, thirty miles off his port bow. He squeezed his eyes shut, opened them and looked again. There it lay—a city, a patterned design in pale pinks and blues and yellows, spread across the gently heaving surface of the deep ocean.

He descended to five thousand, flying a wide circular course, skirting the target, sizing it up. There were copters in the air—he could see the tiny golden machines as mere flecks of reflected sunlight, moving busily to and fro, or setting out at remarkable speed across the water toward the distant mainland—and in the other direction too, toward Europe, and south toward the Venezuelan coast.

Twilight deepened. The sun sank in familiar glory into a molten copper sea; the first stars emerged. Across the island city, lights came on, lining avenues, sparkling from slim towers, winking from circling aircraft. Blondel took a deep breath to quell the roil in his stomach, dropped down until he was riding mere yards above the ghostly whitecaps. It was almost full dark now. He picked a spot that seemed to have less than the usual quota of lights, and headed toward the floating fortress-headquarters of the Monitors.

It was astonishingly easy. The rim of the island rose sheer, ten feet above the choppy seas which seemed to damp out as they approached the barrier before them. Blondel flitted down almost silently in the shadow of a graceful peach-colored dome, settled on a patch of what appeared to be scarlet grass, swiftly slipped out of the confining harness and hobbled on stiff limbs to the concealment of a flowering shrub.

He stretched out, repressing groans of mingled pleasure and pain, massaged his cramped legs and shoulders, half-expecting to be pounced on by a squad of alert Monitors. Through the stems of the bush he could see the lighted avenue a block distant, thronged with slim, athletic figures moving about their business His eye fell on the SCRAG copter, lying where he had left it by a tiled walk, as conspicuous as a dead cat on the parlor rug. He got to his feet, limped to it, his head still hamming from the fourteen hours under the whirling blades, lifted the apparatus and staggered back with it to shove it far back under the foliage. Another glance along the grassy walks and gardens revealed no hordes of traffic cops descending. His approach, it appeared, had been unnoticed.

The next problem was assuming larger proportions now: how to find the commander of the invading forces. There was a large number of imposing towers in sight, any one of which might house the supreme enemy headquarters. His best bet, he reflected, might be simply to appear and let himself be captured, after which . . .

Footsteps crunched gravel nearby. Blondel crouched back, saw a slender figure come into view around a curve in the walk. In the glow of the varicolored lights sprinkled across the nearby buildings, he saw that it was a nicely-stacked young female. She came along slowly, humming to herself. Blondel held his breath as she paused, looking down at the trampled spot where the tiny copter had landed. The girl stooped, came up with a scrap of paper. Blondel winced as he recognized it as a Hershey-bar wrapper, one of those he had emptied during the flight.

The girl turned, following the drag marks Blondel had made in the grass. She lifted the screening fronds aside, peered in at him.

"My God," she said, "what in the world are you doing in there, Blondel?"

"Nelda—I can hardly believe—I mean, you look so—"

"Stop stuttering," the girl said sharply. "So I've lost weight; but inside, I'm still the same ego-Gestalt in confrontation with a cryptic universe."

"It's you, all right," Blondel conceded. "But it's only been a day and a half—"

Nelda waved a slim, manicured hand. "There's nothing miraculous about it; the Monitors have a total understanding of such elementary matters as human metabolism. Pekky arranged for me to have an hour or two in the organic symmetrizer to iron out my little obesity problem. But that's merely superficial. What I flipped over was his understanding of the real, inner, suffering me!"

"That's fine, Nelda," Blondel said nervously. "Ah . . . is he trailing along behind you somewhere?" He looked back along her trail.

Nelda sighed. "No. It's always like this. Every time I find what appears to be a true, fate-ordained relationship, it turns out to be platonic."

"That's too bad," Blondel commiserated, noting the sleek curve of her once bulging flank, the perfectly proportioned swell of her formerly overwhelming bosom. "But I'm sure you're going to make lots of new friends. In the meantime, maybe you could help me—"

"Help you?" Nelda echoed irately. "That's all I'm for, I suppose! I just happened to be conceived, born, nourished, educated, matured and placed in this particular spot just so I could lend you five?"

"Gosh, Nelda, you take a more macrocosmic view of things than I do," Blondel protested. "I just meant—"

"What are you doing here, anyway? Why are you dining behind the shrubbery? You're not one of those poor warped creatures who jump out at girls, are you?"

"Nelda, you know me better than that!"

"Yes—I know you have an irrational prejudice against the Monitors, who just happen to be the most marvelous thing that's ever happened to the human race!"

"Now, Nelda, I'm not prejudiced, but after all—"

"Why, of course," Nelda clapped her hands together, "you've seen the truth at last!"

"Right!" Blondel agreed. "That's why I'm here, and—"

"Blondel, I should have known that such an essentially perceptive person as yourself would eventually wake up to the real nature of the Monitors!"

"You mean—you know, too?"

"Of course. I suspected it the minute I met Pekky, and when I got to know him better—you know—then I was sure!"

Blondel nodded. "I guess that *would* be a dead giveaway."

"I suppose you'll want your synaptic therapy right away; that's best, because then you're so much more receptive to what they call Gross Orientation, which, of course, precedes the *real* re-educational process."

"Hold on, Nelda. I'm not sure—"

"Oh, don't be silly." Nelda took his arm and tugged at him. "There's no point in losing your nerve just before the big moment! There's nothing to be afraid of—"

"Wait! I don't think you understand, Nelda! You mean that even now, after you know what they're really like, that you want to sign up for their programs?"

"Don't *you*?"

"I'd prefer to leave my brains in their present self-scrambled condition, thanks." Blondel disengaged his arm.

"Don't be a total cuboid, Blondel! Come along now, and we'll go find Pekky and ask him to help you."

"I don't want their help! This is a serious matter. Don't you understand?"

"Certainly, I know the old instinct for the inviolability of the psyche. But it's like a lot of other silly old Judeo-Christian hang-ups: After all, the essence of fun is the violation of ritualistic taboos!"

"Nelda, I came here for a purpose—"

"And now we'll see to it that you don't chicken out at the last moment."

Blondel, weak with fatigue, found himself being hauled bodily from hiding.

"Nelda, the future of the human race—"

"That's it, Blondel! The whole, glorious, Monitor-directed future of our poor, helpless, struggling species! All you have to do is relax, and it will all be taken care of!"

Blondel stiffened himself, pulled free from Nelda's grip. "Sure," he panted. "That's the dream of humanity, in a nutshell. But I'm not ready to sign up for embalming yet, not as long as I can still suck in air and blow it out again!"

"Blondel, you cretin! Do you mean you'd reject all the wonderful things the Monitors offer, just because of some idiotic, old-fashioned, *masculine* idea, like that nonsense about climbing mountains and planting flags on top, just because they're there?"

"You name it," Blondel said. "All I know is, I don't want my destiny delivered to my door, gift-wrapped!"

"Men!" Nelda planted her fists on her trim hips. "You need keepers, and we women are lucky the Monitors came along to take you in hand!"

"Now, Nelda, women are men, too, in one sense of the word—"

"We're a race apart," Nelda said flatly. "Well, then, if you didn't come to join the forces of enlightenment, what *do* you want here? How did you get here, anyway? What are you planning to do? Why don't you want them to know you're here?"

"Nelda," Blondel appealed. "Calm yourself. I want to see the leader of the Monitors. He must be here, somewhere."

"You mean the Tersh?"

"Not Jetterax?"

"Certainly. Why do you want to see him?"

"I . . . I have something to tell him."

"Blondel, I don't trust you!"

"How can it hurt anything for me to talk to him?" Blondel spread his hands.

"You aren't planning any . . . any mischief?"

"Who me, Nelda?" Blondel looked innocent. "What could a mere man do to hurt a Monitor?"

"That's true," Nelda conceded. "But why

don't you tell me what it is you want to tell
him?"

"Never mind." Blondel started past her.
"I'll find him myself."

"No, wait; I guess you have to indulge
your boyish taste for the mysterious. Come
on, and we'll see if we can catch him before
mid-morning contemplation."

The Tersh Jetterax looked up, beaming
broadly as Nelda and Blondel appeared at
the open archway that gave entrance to the
airy vine-hung terrace where he sat behind
a low table set with a vast fruit bowl, plates
on doilies, and gleaming silver.

"Ah, welcome, my dears!" he cried. "My
morning is complete, now! Do sit down!
Nelda, how delightful to see the real you,
freed from its former cocoon of unhealthy
flesh. And Blondel! At last you've come to
us!"

"Humph!" Nelda sniffed. "It wasn't so
unhealthy. In fact, some gentlemen prefer a
well-fleshed girl."

"Of course; but it's these weird imbalances we're all pledged to correct, eh? Now,
Blondel, dear boy, I've followed your adventures with considerable interest. In a sense,
your experiences have been a microcosm of
what we must expect to encounter in the
process of correcting all the faults of your
charming little world."

"You've, er, followed my adventures?"

The Tersh nodded. "And how delighted I was when I saw that at last you were turning your course here. Your disillusionment was a difficult time for you; but I fancy that now, as you enter your new, enriched life, the old traumas will soon disappear, and—"

"I wonder," Blondel interrupted, "if I could have a few words with you in private?"

"Eh? But what have we to conceal, my boy? The suspicions and mutual mistrusts which once made such subterfuge necessary do not exist here—"

"I have to talk to you alone."

"You mean you want me to leave?" Nelda fumed. "Well, of all the—and after I brought you here myself—"

"Perhaps it would be best to indulge our new guest's wishes," the Tersh suggested gently. "Just for a short while, Nelda. There's a dear child."

She departed, protesting. Blondel took the chair across from the aged-looking Monitor.

"Now, Blondel, in what way can I serve you?" The latter beamed.

"Skip the routine," Blondel said bluntly. "I know what you are."

The Tersh eyed him almost blankly, his wrinkled features twitching into a number of tentative expressions before falling back into the bland smile.

"Don't bother with the grimaces," Blondel said. "It must be a strain on you, running through a list of native facial codes and then working the right levers. I'd rather have you conserve your energy for what I have to tell you."

"Ah . . . are you feeling well, my boy?"

"*Your* boy probably has nine legs and tentacles," Blondel said bluntly. "I don't know where you come from, but we can cover that later—if there is a 'later.' Right now I have an ultimatum to deliver."

There was a short, strained silence. Then: "This is unfortunate," the Tersh said. "I see that you have somehow stumbled on a small item of information that I had hoped to keep confidential for just a little longer. Yes, we Monitors are not members of your own race; but, believe me, we *are* your friends."

"Why the masquerade, then? Why not come slithering up to us, monster to man, and make your pitch?"

"I considered that the donning of cosmetic prosthetics was no more than courteous," the Tersh Jetterax said in a dignified tone. "After all, in your present immature state of xenophobia you were hardly prepared to deal with nonhumans as potential friends."

"How true. Now that we've got that straightened out, how long will it take you to pack up and scat back to your home base?"

"Now, now, Blondel, don't be hasty." The Tersh showed a patient smile. "Surely you can see that for our mission to depart now would be a gross injustice to your poor race?''

"Nuts," Blondel dismissed the proposition. "What have you done that's so great? Cleared out a few slums, straightened out the highways, fired some crooked cops, and taken the fat off some of our compulsive eaters. Not a thing we couldn't have done ourselves!"

"But *did* you do them?" the Tersh murmured. "As for more sophisticated measures, to introduce any technique from a higher technological plateau would be a gross violation of regulations." He shook his head. "No, my boy, our obligation to the entire brotherhood of intelligent life permits of no move so barbaric as to leave you to your own devices now. No matter how petty, cruel, blind, shortsighted, foolish, venal, bloodthirsty, masochistic and obtuse you may be, it is a matter of principle with us, as civilized beings, to do our very best to raise you to our own level of advancement along the road to true enlightenment."

"Too bad," Blondel said shortly. "You have just twenty-four hours to clear out."

"Now, now, dear boy—"

"If you're as fast on your feet leaving as you were arriving, that shouldn't strain your capabilities."

"Please, Blondel, don't create unnecessary patterns of frustration within your already confused psyche—"

"The twenty-four hours have already started," Blondel said curtly. "You have twenty-three hours, fifty-nine minutes, and thirty seconds left."

The Tersh sighed. "I do wish that I could prevail on you to voluntarily undergo remedial treatment, Blondel. It would clear up any number of erroneous reaction-patterns—"

"I don't need any lobotomies performed by interstellar do-gooders," Blondel cut him off. "You'd better get started giving the orders to pull out."

"Surely you realize the futility of attempting to browbeat me," the Tersh said, almost sternly.

"I'm not browbeating you. I'm threatening you. Pack up and get out, or I'll blow this whole raft to kingdom come!"

The Tersh smiled sadly. "You must be aware by now that violence is ineffective against us. Our automatic protective screens repel all potentially unstable molecules, both chemical and nuclear. No weapon can enter here. And if it did, the nature of our defenses is such that any force applied is merely turned back against the attacker."

"No weapon, eh? What would you say if I told you there *was* such a weapon—and that I control it? A weapon that would make a nuclear bomb look like a toy?"

The Tersh stiffened. "I wouldn't believe you."

"Ever heard of an implosion bomb?" Blondel asked flatly.

"An . . . implosion bomb?"

"That's right. Implosion bomb."

"No . . . I can't say that I have."

"Picture it," Blondel invited grimly. "A five-mile-wide bubble of perfect vacuum, all rushing in toward a central core of annihilated matter. The defensive fields will help the reaction along: they'll be triggered, but in reverse; instead of bouncing back an attack from outside, they'll reinforce the collapse from within. In a split microsecond your whole headquarters will be one big slag bubble, smashed flatter than a boardinghouse pancake."

"I . . . I don't understand. . . ."

"The end will come in its ghastliest form," Blondel pressed on. "Picture it, Jetterax: The Ultimate Closure. . . ."

The Tersh made a small yipping sound and shrank back in his chair. For a moment his pseudohuman limbs quivered, uncontrolled. His mask drooped to an expression of idiot vacuity.

"That's the picture," Blondel bored on relentlessly. "Get out or get flattened. You've got twenty-three hours and fifty-eight minutes left."

"*Ukkkk!*" Jetterax croaked. "*Ikkkkk! Rrrr-mmmmm!*" He shook himself, with an obvious effort brought his shuddering members under control. His face worked, then froze into a horrified grimace.

"You'd ... you'd do this ... this hideous thing? To us—who brought you only good, who meant only kindness and love?"

"Yep."

"But ... but how could you doubt our benign intentions? Haven't we proved already that we are kindly, tolerant—"

"The human race refuses to be tolerated," Blondel told him. "Your visit has had one beneficial effect—and I don't mean the pretty flowers. In time, we'd have gotten around to all that ourselves. You've made it pretty clear to us that there's a Galactic Culture out there and we've been tossed into it, ready or not. And humanity being what it is, we'll enter the club as first-class members on our own efforts—or not at all."

"But think, Blondel! By accepting us as your leaders you could save generations of heartbreaking effort, centuries of human suffering, millennia of trial-and-error—"

"And end up as Galactic lap-dogs. No thanks, Jetterax. We'll do it alone. That's the way we are; anything we haven't worked for, we don't appreciate."

The Tersh straightened. "I see you are in earnest," he said hollowly. "Your tragic folly will bring nothing but pain and destruction, where there could have been sunshine and joy. Well, then, proceed, my boy! Bring on your bomb—if your threat was not idle! Blast me and my faithful workers into nothingness! But even if you destroy us all it will avail you nothing. All missionary services expect casualties. A new Tersh will come out to replace me, and the work will go on. With the help of your people or without it, we will civilize you in the end. And one day your descendants will thank us, and rue the unnecessary violence that preceded the millennium."

"Now, wait a minute," Blondel protested. "I'm not bluffing! The bomb exists, and it's already planted where it will do the most good, and—"

"I believe you," the Tersh said mildly. "Your race's capacity for violence exceeds anything we have heretofore encountered. And such a weapon as you describe would, in truth, penetrate our shields undetected and turn our own defenses against us. I concede it all. And I say—proceed, if you must. A few Monitorial lives are small payment for the salvation of a savage race."

"But—you were supposed to . . . I mean, *I'm* the one giving the orders!"

"I defy you, Blondel." Jetterax drew himself up. "We Monitors, too, know how to die."

"I don't want you to die!" Blondel yelped. "I want you to surrender and go back home!"

"Never."

"Never?"

"Not ever."

"But in the movies—"

"This, my boy, is not a movie."

Blondel stared glumly across at the alien. His shoulders drooped. He sighed.

"I should have known nothing Blackwish had anything to do with would work," he said. He reached in his pocket, took out the heavy cylindrical implosion bomb, placed it gently on the table.

"Here," he said. "You win. Get rid of this thing before it hurts somebody."

"Isn't it marvelous?" Nelda cooed, clinging to Blondel's arm as they strolled beside a rippling brook flowing across the crimson-carpeted park that lay among the cherry-bright towers of the island fortress. "I just knew that everything was going to work out perfectly, after the Tersh made such a generous, wonderful gesture!"

"Well, maybe it will help a little," Blondel said glumly. "Putting local human bosses into all the second-string administrative jobs will at least give us an illusion that we're running our own business."

"It was just the sort of kind, thoughtful, *darling* thing you'd expect from him!"

"Umph." Blondel plodded along in silence for a few yards. "I guess I'd better be getting back to the mainland," he said. "After wading around in all this sweetness and light for the past three days, I'm ready for a change."

"Ace, dear, if only you wouldn't be such an old reactionary about having your synaptic treatment," Nelda chided, "you'd shed all these primordial competitive urges and settle down to enrich the garden of your mind with the heady fertilizer of Monitorial wisdom."

"A head full of fertilizer isn't what I'm yearning for at the moment." Blondel paused to kick at a pale-pink daisy nodding in the gentle summery breeze. "I think I'll find myself a spot up in the mountains some-where, with lots of nice trees and a trout stream, and build myself a little log cabin, and plant a small garden patch, and start tanning my own hides and making fishhooks out of antlers, and getting back to nature."

"My God," Nelda said mildly. "Your asociality is burgeoning into a full-fledged neurosis."

"I'm not completely asocial," Blondel corrected. "For example, I had an idea . . . that is, I thought maybe, ah, you might like to go along."

"Me?"

"Sure." Blondel patted the sleek curve of her rump. "I—"

Nelda's roundhouse swing caught him squarely across the side of the head, sent him staggering back, eyes watering, bright lights whirling before him.

"Keep your lascivious, grasping hands to yourself, *Mister* Blondel!" she shrilled.

"But . . . but Nelda! Have you forgotten what a nice, friendly relationship we had—"

"Fooie." She tossed her head, and even through the pain tears Blondel admired the graceful line of her remodelled throat and chin, the bright haze of her blonde hair, the vivacious curve of her pouty red lips. "That was *before*."

"Yes, but I thought you said that inside, you're the same poor, lonely, suffering you!"

"New packaging, new rules, Blondel," Nelda said carelessly. "Now, you may escort me, if you promise to be a gentleman."

"Gentleman?" Blondel echoed numbly.

"And if you're a very, very good boy, I may let you have just one, teensy, little kiss—later."

"Well," Blondel fell in beside her, "you've got to start somewhere."

"Mr. Blondel!" He turned at an agitated shout from across the velvety lawn. "Mr. Blondel, come quickly! The Tersh needs you! Something terrible has happened!"

"It's simply incredible," the Tersh Jetterax wailed, wringing his imitation hands in a practiced gesture. "In all my years of experience I've never before seen such an outburst of insanity! The entire population of the planet seems to have been seized by a frenzy! Riots are sweeping every center of population larger than a two-family house! My Monitors have been mobbed, their defensive screens overwhelmed by sheer weight of numbers! Wild-eyed hordes have beaten them and herded them into improvised concentration camps! Everything we've done— all of our programs, our orientation centers, our retraining classes—all disrupted; our instructors sent fleeing, our timetables shattered into total chaos! *Why? Why?*"

Blondel, reading the reports coming in over the small TV screen on the Tersh's desk, nodded.

"It looks as though it's a toss-up between disappointed jobseekers out to fill the new bureaucratic slots, and the rank and file who resent having some dull clod of a colorless neighbor put in charge of them. Between the two categories, I guess they constitute about ninety-seven per cent of the population. The other three per cent is joining in out of sheer animal spirits."

"Never did I dream that I would see the day when the rule of peace and good-fellowship would fail," the Tersh said in a dull, defeated voice. "I was prepared to persevere through any imaginable setback; but to find the entire planetary population united as one in a frenzy of total resistance—this is too much."

"Well, being told what to do by an obviously superior being is one thing," Blondel pointed out. "Taking orders from the idiot next door is something no red-blooded American boy could stand for. And I guess the same thing goes for red-blooded Poles, Welshmen, Masais, and Lower Laplanders."

"I admit defeat," the Tersh said in a sepulchral voice. "My Monitors will leave immediately."

"Now, wait just a minute," Blondel said.

"Don't do anything hasty. Let's talk this over first."

"Nothing remains to be said, Blondel. The reports speak for themselves."

"Send your boys out somewhere to rake leaves." Blondel indicated the group of worried Monitors standing anxiously by. "You and I need to have another little conference."

"It was the only sensible thing to do," Blondel told Nelda as they sat together on a marblelike bench overlooking a superb sunset. "After all, it's pretty obvious that running a planet is a job that takes certain skills. Letting amateurs try to handle it is pretty idiotic, when there's a corps of specialists around willing to take on the chore."

"Yes, certainly—but I thought you were against all that! What about your ideas that man's poor little psyche would wither on the vine if he wasn't strutting around on top of the heap, bossing everything?"

"Oh, he is, he is." Blondel waved the heavy roll of parchment in his hand. "The contract clearly spells out that the Monitors are employed by the human race as governmental specialists, empowered to do whatever they find necessary to keep everything running smoothly. Nobody minds listening to advice from experts, as long as the experts are clearly in an inferior position, liable to being summarily fired if they fail to please."

"Contract government!" Nelda marveled. "Well, it's something new. But who authorized you to sign a contract with an extraterrestial power?"

"I appointed myself Human Ambassador to the Monitors," Blondel said, "and Commissioner of Extraterrestrial Affairs. I guess that gives me rank enough to handle the job."

"But isn't that a pretty arrogant usurpation of power? I mean, why don't you call an election—"

"The contract doesn't call for any more nonsense," Blondel said. "From now on things will be done according to plan."

"But will people accept that?"

"People only ignore free advice. When they pay enough for it, they follow it to the letter."

"How are we paying? What have we got that the Monitors need?"

"They seem to find our art work quite vigorous, in a primitive, undisciplined way. We'll have to set up a big new art program, to let all our frustrated geniuses develop their talents; but that's right in line with the program."

"My God." Nelda shook her head. "So many changes, all at once. How are we going to keep our bearings in such a total cultural turmoil? I have a sudden apprehension that we're all going to flip our wigs in sheer disorientation at the reshuffling of traditional values. . . ."

"Never mind." Blondel tentatively gained

another inch in his campaign to insinuate his arm around Nelda's slim waist. He tilted her chin up and smiled into her bright blue eyes. "There are still a few old habits that we can cling to—purely for reasons of mental health, of course."

"Purely?" Nelda murmured, and nibbled his ear.

"Well, maybe just a little bit just for the hell of it." Blondel admitted, and together they slid off the bench to a softer resting place among the pink daisies.